"TRACKER...TRACKER..."

she moaned, feeling the perspiration roll down her face. A drop paused on the tip of her nose and Tracker licked it off. It was such a simple, easy thing to do, yet it seemed to increase the sensations...no man had ever done to her the things that Tracker had done...was doing.

"Tracker, I can't take it...we have to stop."

"Stop?" he asked. "You mean you've had enough?"

"Yes, damn it!" she snapped, almost desperately. "I surrender...I never thought I'd ever say this to a man—oh, Jesus!—but I've had enough..." And then after the space of one heartbeat she added,

"That is, for now..."

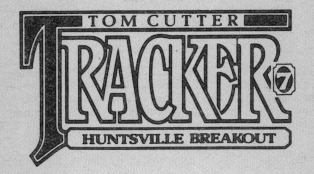

TOM CUTTER

TRACKER 7

HUNTSVILLE BREAKOUT

AVON
PUBLISHERS OF BARD, CAMELOT, DISCUS AND FLARE BOOKS

TRACKER 7: HUNTSVILLE BREAKOUT is an original publication of Avon Books. This work has never before appeared in book form. This work is a novel. Any similarity to actual persons or events is purely coincidental.

AVON BOOKS
A division of
The Hearst Corporation
1790 Broadway
New York, New York 10019

Copyright © 1985 by Robert J. Randisi
Published by arrangement with the author
Library of Congress Catalog Card Number: 84-091262
ISBN: 0-380-89584-6

First Avon Printing, June 1985

AVON TRADEMARK REG. U. S. PAT. OFF. AND IN OTHER COUNTRIES, MARCA REGISTRADA, HECHO EN U. S. A.

Printed in the U. S. A.

WFH   10   9   8   7   6   5   4   3   2   1

To MICHAEL SEIDMAN

[1]

Farrell House was by no means the fanciest hotel in San Francisco. In fact, it was not even located in Portsmouth Square, where the fancy gambling house-cum-hotels were located, but rather was about two blocks off the Square. So it didn't have the stature of, say, the Alhambra or the Bella Union, or the Varsouvienne. It had, however, flourished and grown under the direction of a man named Duke Farrell who, in spite of the fact that he had named the hotel, did not own it. Instead, he managed the place and "fronted" for one of the owners who preferred to remain in the background. During the nearly two years he had held that position, profits had risen, and clientele had improved. Farrell House could now claim as some of its past guests royalty in the persons of a Russian Countess, an English Duke and Duchess, and Happy O'Toole, self-proclaimed King of the Leprechauns.

The man who entered the lobby of Farrell House that morning was not royalty by any means. He was a portly, gray-haired man who carried a bowler hat in his hands as he approached the front desk, which was being tended by Shana Sullivan.

"Can I help you?" she asked him pleasantly.

The man looked at her nervously, rotating his hat in his pudgy hands and said, "Uh, yes, I'd like to see a man named Tracker, please."

"So would I," Shana muttered beneath her breath. The fiery redhead was a frequent bed partner of Tracker's, but had not been alone with the big man for some three days, now. Shana wondered if Deirdre Long didn't have something to do with that.

"Excuse me?" the man asked, thinking she was addressing him.

"Oh, nothing. Someone will be out to talk with you shortly."

"Tracker," the man said again.

"Yeah, sure. Have a seat."

Shana knew the drill when someone came in to talk to Tracker. She still didn't know exactly what Tracker did to make his money, but she did know that nobody got to see him without seeing Duke first.

She collared a bellhop and sent him to look for Duke. The portly man kept looking up at her nervously, and she kept flashing him a smile she hoped would increase his patience.

"Shana," Duke said suddenly, from behind her.

"There you are," she said, turning to face him. Shana was several inches taller than Duke and she had to lower her gaze to meet his eyes.

"That him?"

"Yes."

"He looks nervous. What did you do to him?"

"I smiled at him."

"That'd make any man nervous."

"He came in that way," she said, making a face at him. "He stumbled over his words and asked for Tracker."

"All right. I'll see to him."

"Where is Tracker, anyway?"

He looked at her and said, "I wish I knew, since I may need him in the next few minutes. See if you can locate him, will you?"

"Ask him to come here?"

"No, just find out where he is, just in case I need him."

"Right."

Tracker was in his room at that moment, and not alone. Deirdre Long's feelings for Tracker were extreme: She either loved him or hated him. This was one of the loving times.

When she was in Tracker's bed—or he in hers—she could think of nothing else; she was overwhelmed by him. When he was gone she would become angry with

8

herself for being affected by him in that way. She was a very individual, independent person—except when she was with him; and the fact that he had to come to her rescue in Oklahoma a couple of months before didn't help her self-image, either.

Now they were together, though, and she cared only for his lips, roaming about her body; his teeth, nibbling her nipples; his hands, squeezing and probing and caressing her...

...And then her hands were raking his back and her strong legs were wrapped around his waist as he drove himself deeply into her and pulled her closer to him with his large hands palming her smooth buttocks...

...And then somebody knocked on the door.

"Damn!" Deirdre said.

"That's not very ladylike," Tracker said, scolding her. "Don't answer it."

"If I don't answer it we'll end up rushing this," he said, "and I don't want to do that."

"Ohhh!" she moaned as he withdrew his swollen cock from her slick grasp.

"Hold my place, I'll be right back."

He put his jeans on and went to answer the door, barechested and barefoot.

"Uh, I interrupted something, didn't I?" Duke asked.

"Good guess," Tracker said. At six-foot-four he towered over the smaller con man–turned–hotel manager, who was one of the few men in the world that Tracker liked and respected. "Is there a problem I should know about?"

"Not a problem, exactly," Duke said, making no effort to peek past Tracker to see who was in the room with him. He was pretty sure he knew that.

"Then what?"

"There's a man downstairs who wants to see you."

Tracker's eyebrows went up. He asked, "Money?"

Duke gave a little I-don't-know shrug with his shoulders and handed Tracker an envelope.

"What's this?"

"It's got *your* name on it."

Tracker nodded and unsealed it. The envelope held money, and what seemed to be a lot of it.

Tracker showed it to Duke who whistled soundlessly and asked, "How much?"

"Four, maybe five thousand."

"For what?"

Tracker gave Duke a hard look and said, "That's what I was going to ask you."

"Don't look at me. I talked to the man for a while, Tracker. He won't say why he wants to talk to you, or who he is."

"Well, what *did* he say?"

"He said that what was in the envelope was yours if you talked to him."

"Just talk?"

Again Duke shrugged.

"What's he like?"

"Nervous, tense; he's not acting for himself. Somebody sent him."

Tracker tapped the palm of his hand with the envelope and said, "Now you've really got my curiosity up."

"I think that was the whole point."

Tracker thought a moment, then said, "Well, all I've got to say is that it better be worth it."

"Should I put him in the office?"

"Yeah. Tell him I'll be down..."

"When?" Duke prompted when Tracker paused.

Thinking about Deirdre Tracker said, "Let him stew a while. Tell him I'll be down...directly."

"Gotcha."

Tracker closed the door, slid out of his jeans and went back to Deirdre.

"Something tells me," she said, watching Tracker walk to the bed, "that we're going to have to rush anyway."

"Not a chance in the world," the big man said, and set about to prove it.

Deirdre rose up to meet him and he cupped her firm breasts as his mouth closed over hers. She slid her arms around him and bore him down onto the bed with her full weight. He was such a big man, yet he never seemed to crush her. It sometimes surprised her to find how considerate he was of her needs when they were together.

His penis had lost none of its rigidity during the interruption, and she had lost none of her readiness, and he slid into her easily and fully. They began slowly until their rhythm matched and then built to the point where their passion was almost mindless. When they both climaxed the release was almost a relief, and it left them both gasping.

"My God," Deirdre said, breathlessly, "what would it have been like if we took our time?"

He kissed her and said, "Wait here for me and we'll find out."

She smiled, but said, "No, I can't. I have to go to work."

"I happen to know that neither of the owners would mind if you waited here."

"You're going to be busy," she said, "and this owner would mind. It's important to me that I work this hotel as well as own it, Tracker."

"All right," he said. "We'll find out another time."

As he got up off the bed and started to get dressed she asked, "How about tonight?"

He grinned and said, "I'll meet you here."

[2]

When the door to the office opened and Tracker stepped in Duke instinctively got up to leave. He may have fronted for Tracker and screened his callers, but he was not privy to the big man's business arrangements.

"Mr. Bishop, this is Tracker," he said, on his way to the door. "I'll leave the two of you alone with your business."

As he passed Tracker in the doorway he said, "I've had conversations with clams that were more enlightening."

Tracker nodded, and closed the door behind him. He walked to the desk, where he dropped the envelope of money, seated himself behind it and regarded the portly, gray-haired man stonily. Already aware of the fact that the man seemed nervous, he had decided to play on that trait and use it to his advantage.

"I'd like you to explain this, please," he said finally, indicating the envelope on the desk.

"I should think that it was self-explanatory," the man said, mopping his face with a blue kerchief. It was not particularly warm in the office.

"Nobody gives away four or five thousand—"

"Excuse me, it's five."

"Nobody *gives* away five thousand dollars for a few moments of my time, Mr. Bishop. Who do you represent?"

"I'm afraid I'm not at liberty to divulge that, Mr. Tracker, but I'm sure you'll find what I have to say very interesting, because it does amount to giving five thousand dollars away for ... nothing."

"You'll have to explain that one to me, Mr. Bishop."

"Precisely why I'm here, sir."

"I'm listening," Tracker said, pinning the man with a hard stare.

"My principal is prepared to pay you that five thousand dollars to do nothing."

"You're still talking in riddles, Bishop, and I'm getting tired of it."

"Uh, yes, I'll explain further." The man took a moment to collect his thoughts—and mop his face again—and then said, "In the next few days you will be approached by a man from the bank of Huntsville, Texas. He will offer you a job."

"What kind of job?"

"That doesn't matter," Bishop said, shaking his head. "What matters is that you take our money, and not the man's job."

"Is that a fact? You want me to take five thousand dollars to do nothing."

"Exactly."

"I'll be very blunt, Bishop, and then we can go our separate ways. I make my money by working, and I enjoy what I do. I do not take money to do nothing."

"I—I don't think you understand," Bishop said, frowning. "That's five thousand dollars."

"I haven't counted it," Tracker said, picking up the envelope and tossing it into the man's lap, "but I'm willing to take your word for it. Take that back to the man you work for and tell him no deal."

Bishop picked the envelope up and tucked it away inside his jacket, frowning all the while.

"I believe I'll have to make one more effort—"

"Don't," Tracker said, holding his hand out so that the man could see his palm. "I could probably pick you up with one hand and go through your pockets with the other, Bishop, and maybe come up with something that would tell me who you work for, but I'm not going to do that."

The man looked frightened, and then relieved as Tracker finished his statement.

"I could change my mind, however," Tracker continued, "so I suggest that you leave now before that happens. Nobody here is interested in your proposal."

Tracker stood up slowly and the nervous man nearly jumped to his feet and backed his way to the door.

"I will relay your message—"

"You do that."

Bishop continued to back his way to the door, as if afraid that Tracker might suddenly leap at him from behind the desk. He groped behind him for the doorknob with one hand while clutching his damp blue kerchief with the other, and when he got it open he hurried through it and shut it behind him.

A few moments later Duke came into the office and found Tracker still standing behind the desk.

"My curiosity would never forgive me if I didn't ask," Duke said to the big man. "Of course, you don't have to answer—"

"He wanted to give me five thousand dollars to do nothing."

"Why can't I ever get offers like that?"

Tracker explained the meeting to Duke—something he had seldom done before, but since it hadn't resulted in a job, he made an exception.

"Why *didn't* you shake the name of his employer out of him?" Duke wondered aloud.

"I didn't have to," Tracker answered, simply. "There'll be a follow-up visit," he said, coming around from behind the desk. "There would have to be."

[3]

The next visit occurred the following day, and began much the same way. A man presented himself to Shana at the desk and announced that he would like to see Tracker, who was easier to locate this time. He was in the hotel saloon talking to the bartender, Will Sullivan, who was Shana's brother.

Duke placed the man in the office and found Tracker in the saloon.

"So soon?" Tracker asked, reading the look on Duke's face correctly.

"He's waiting in the office."

"No envelope this time?"

Duke shook his head.

"Well, this could be the visit that Bishop was talking about yesterday, rather than a second visit from his people."

"I don't know what you're talking about," Will Sullivan said, "but whatever it is, seems to me there's only one way to find out."

"Right," Tracker said, picking up the remainder of his beer, "by talking to the man." He drained the glass. "See you later."

When Tracker entered the office the man waiting there stood up and turned to meet him. That was the first thing that differentiated him from Bishop, yesterday's visitor. From there on, the differences came in obvious bunches.

This man was tall and slender, in very good shape for a man in his late forties or early fifties. His hair was black with some gray on the sides, and he was wearing a three-piece suit—and although the suit itself did not stamp him as a man of means, the *way* he wore

15

it did. He was the kind of man who could sleep in a suit like that, and still look neat as a pin the next morning. Tracker had worn a three-piece suit once or twice since taking up residence in San Francisco, and he always felt like a mule trying to look like a horse.

"I'm Tracker," he said to the man, getting right to the point. "And you are..."

"My name is William Jeffery," the man said, reaching inside his jacket for something. "My credentials." He handed Tracker a card that identified him as an officer of the Bank of Huntsville, Texas.

Tracker handed it back and said, "What can I do for you...or for the Bank of Huntsville?"

"You were recommended to us as a reliable investigator—" the man began, but Tracker cut him off quickly, to dispel any wrong notions.

"Someone gave you the wrong information, Mr. Jeffery"

"Is that so?"

"Yes, it is," Tracker said. "I'm not an investigator, and I never have been."

"Perhaps I used the wrong word," Jeffery admitted. "How would you describe yourself?"

Tracker thought a moment, then decided on an appropriate description of the way he made his living.

"I'd call myself a recovery agent."

"So be it," Jeffery said. "That's just what we need, and you were recommended as reliable."

"That's comforting."

"Yes," Jeffery said, as if he thought it should be.

"What's missing?"

"Money."

"That comes as no surprise," Tracker said. "How much money are we talking about?"

"A...tidy sum," Jeffery hedged. "We can discuss that in a moment."

"Why not now?"

Jeffery set his lips.

"Your normal fee is, I believe, half of what you recover," the banker said.

"That's right," Tracker said, impressed with the man's knowledge of how he operated. As a rule, Tracker never asked a potential client where they had gotten his name, but now he quite frankly wondered.

"That would be quite out of line in this case," Jeffery said. "We would hope that you would...modify your regular fee in this instance and perhaps consent to accepting ten percent."

"Ten percent?" Tracker asked, shaking his head. "I've never worked for ten percent before. We must be talking about more than a tidy sum here, Mr. Jeffery. Could we dispense with the secrecy and get to it?"

The man seemed to steel himself, and then nodded and said, "Very well. We lost six hundred thousand dollars."

$600,000!

Tracker thought about that for a few moments and realized that the bank would have to be desperate to pay him half of that. If he accepted the ten percent, that still left him—in Jeffery's words—a tidy sum of $60,000.

Before he accepted, however, he decided to feel Jeffery out and see just how desperate the bank really was.

"Why did the bank have so much money on hand?" he asked.

Though Jeffery looked uncomfortable about discussing it, he knew that it was necessary and launched into a monotone explanation.

"The Huntsville Prison—which I'm sure you've heard of—has a very large staff and, in addition to the normal bank receipts for the two businesses, the thieves got away with the Huntsville Penitentiary payroll."

"There must be quite a few angry guards in Texas."

"Not to mention the warden. It's going to take some time to replace that money."

"I can imagine."

"Eventually, of course, the money *will* be replaced, but the bank has its reputation to consider. A reward has been offered—"

"Ten percent?"

"Yes."

"A reward is collected only when something is recovered," Tracker said. "What do I get if I don't find a cent?"

Jeffery looked surprised and said, "I was under the impression that you were only paid if you made successful recovery."

"I was under the impression that my fee was fifty percent. If I'm making modifications in my normal routine, I think it's only fair that the bank does the same."

"Does that mean that you'll take the job?"

"If we can come to terms."

"What do you suggest?"

"I want a thousand a week guaranteed."

"For how many weeks?"

Tracker thought a moment and then said, "Four. If I don't recover the money in a month, the bank is out four thousand dollars."

Jeffery looked unhappy.

"You'll still be out six hundred thousand," Tracker reminded Jeffery. "Four more, more or less, isn't going to break the bank."

Jeffery still looked unhappy, but Tracker knew that if the man really wanted him to take the job he'd go for the thousand a week. If Tracker recovered the money, the bank's reputation would be salvaged, and Tracker would have made $64,000. Tracker had already decided that if reputation was the problem, and not the money, he wouldn't be able to hold Jeffery up for half the $600,000. He was willing to settle for $64,000.

"Well?" he prompted the banker.

"You have a deal, Mr. Tracker."

"A thousand dollars a week guaranteed, and ten percent of anything I recover?"

"Yes."

"I'll have an agreement drawn up."

"An agreement? I wasn't aware that was a practice of yours."

"It's not," Tracker said, "but then I've never dealt with a bank before."

[4]

"Tracker?" Heck Thomas asked. "Doesn't he have a first name?"

"I suppose he does," longhaired Jim Courtright said, "but we ain't been able to find it."

Heck Thomas was Chief Agent for the Texas Express Company, while Courtright was Chief of Police of Fort Worth, Texas. Thomas had started out as a railroad guard for the company, but had quickly worked his way to detective, and now to Chief Agent. Much of what he had learned about the law, and enforcing it, he had learned from Courtright.

"Well, he's got a reputation, I'll tell you that much," Courtright said.

"As what?"

"He used to be a bounty hunter. Near as we can figure, he's for hire now, mainly to recover stolen property."

"He's not hunting men anymore?"

"Not unless he has to. I hear he keeps fifty percent of whatever he recovers, so I guess he wouldn't balk at hunting down a man to get it."

"Half of six hundred thousand dollars?"

"I doubt that," Courtright said. "No, my guess is that the bank has offered him a fee, maybe ten percent of what he recovers, and I doubt a man like Tracker would turn that down."

"He'd be a fool to."

"He's not a fool, I can tell you that."

"Maybe not, but he ain't getting to that money before me, Jim," Thomas said, standing up. They were in Courtright's office, and Thomas had gotten what he came for—information on what the bank was doing to recover its money. "There's a reward for that money, and the Texas Express Company is going to collect it."

"Meaning you."

"Meaning I'll get a piece of it, yes," Heck Thomas admitted. "But that money was stolen from Texas, Jim, and it'll be recovered by the Texas Express Company."

"Still looking to build a reputation, Heck?" Courtright asked, looking amused. The old man knew that Thomas hungered for some recognition.

"If it comes," Heck Thomas said, "I'll take it."

Thomas started for the door, then turned and said to Courtright, "Appreciate your help, Jim."

"It's always there, Heck. You know that."

"Yeah, I do," Thomas said. "I'll be seeing you."

"I'm sure. Bring a bottle next time."

"I'll do that."

Heck Thomas left the building that housed the Fort Worth Police Department with no new ideas about how to find that damned money. All he'd learned was that the bank had hired their own man to try and find it. If Tracker *did* find the money it might end up costing the bank more, but they'd save face, which was something that was very important to the Bank of Huntsville.

Well, this man Tracker would have to go a long way and then some to get to that money before Heck Thomas.

Thomas only wished that he had some hint about where to look.

[5]

As he rode into Huntsville, Texas, Tracker's mind was still back in San Francisco.

Tracker had explained his absence only to Duke, telling him just what he absolutely needed to know. To Deirdre and Shana, he was simply leaving town on another job.

His last night in town Deirdre had been unavailable, having some hotel business to attend to with Duke, so it was Shana Sullivan that he spent the night with, and in order to avoid any interruptions, they went to her place.

There were no wasted words when they arrived in her room. They simply undressed each other and set about enjoying themselves. Shana was somewhat less inhibited than Deirdre, and also expected no words of undying love or commitment from Tracker. Deirdre didn't expect them either; but the blonde *hoped* for them, and the redhead did not. Tracker had never had a "steady" woman in his lifetime until he came to San Francisco, and he was the most shocked to find that he now had two—although this didn't preclude him from enjoying others. Both Shana and Deirdre knew that they had to share Tracker's attentions with other women, but each also knew that her only serious competition was the other.

"I wonder..." Shana said during a rest period.

"Wonder what?"

"I wonder if Deirdre and I had both been off tonight who you'd be in bed with."

"Those are the kinds of questions I'm real careful never to answer."

21

"I know," she said, laughing softly and turning toward him, "but I don't really care. You're here, which is all that matters."

She opened her mouth and closed it over his, probing with her tongue. He slid his hands over the globes of her smooth buttocks and pulled her hard against him, trapping his massive erection between them. She moaned into his mouth and rubbed her body against his, scraping her nipples against his chest hair, causing them to tingle and swell. Tracker broke the kiss and ran his lips over her neck and shoulders while she gasped for breath. She moved her legs so that she was able to capture his swollen cock between her thighs, and then began to roll it there. He yanked it free so that he could move down further and start nibbling her breasts and nipples. She rolled onto her back, spreading her arms out on both sides and simply giving herself up to the sensations Tracker's hands and mouth were causing.

While sucking on her nipples Tracker inserted two fingers inside her slick, juicy womanhood and used his thumb to manipulate her sensitive nub. Lifting her hips to meet the pressure of his fingers, she moaned aloud and clasped the back of his head, crushing his face against her luscious breasts.

Finally he abandoned her breasts, removed his hand from her crotch and kissed his way down her body until he could bury his tongue inside her, cupping her buttocks in his hands. The taste of her was like honey to a bear and he couldn't get enough. She brought her thighs up and tightened them against his ears, trapping his head there between her legs, where he wanted to be.

He continued to lave her eagerly with his tongue and then finally flicked at her swollen clit, causing her to gasp aloud and tighten her fists against the sheets. He swirled his tongue around her core a few times and then nibbled her, first with his lips, and then with his teeth, until her head was thrashing back and forth on the pillow and she was begging him, pleading with him never to stop. He felt her belly begin to tremble and knew that she was only seconds from completion. He tightened his hold on her buttocks and sucked on her until she began to shout, "Oh yes, that's it, Tracker, that's it..."

She writhed beneath him, as if trying to escape from him, but they both knew better than that. She was simply doing her best to withstand the sensations coursing through her body, without dying!

Later Shana showed just how uninhibited and committed to enjoying sex she was. She moved down between Tracker's legs and began to run her tongue over his shaft and balls. As he had done with her, she slid her hands beneath him to cup his buttocks and continued to lick him until his massive erection gleamed with her saliva. She took the head of his penis into her mouth, feeling the tiny slit with the tip of her tongue, and then slowly allowed more of him to enter her mouth. Then she removed her hands from his buttocks, cradling his balls in one and wrapping the other around the base of his erection. She remained that way for some time, sucking enthusiastically on him until she could feel him pulsating, dangerously close to release. She released him momentarily so she could run her tongue up and down the length of him, bringing a loud groan of pleasure from him. Finally, she took him in her mouth again and brought him to the brink of exploding.

"Jesus, Shana—" he gasped.

She gave a small laugh with him still in her mouth, and then he was filling her mouth with his seed. She took every drop he had to give, then continued to suck on his still-hard shaft, as she wanted more and wouldn't stop until she got it....

Still later, in the middle of the night, Tracker left Shana's room, despite her protests, to go back to the hotel to get *some* sleep before leaving in the morning.

That morning, before leaving, he spoke with Deirdre in the office.

"I'm sorry I was busy last night," she said, "but I'm sure you weren't lonely."

"Deirdre—"

"All right, never mind that," she said, before he could

23

go on. "I just didn't want you to leave without saying goodbye."

"I wouldn't do that," he told her.

"I know."

She moved into the circle of his powerful arms, marveling again at how gentle he was when he held her, and reached up to draw his head down. His kiss thrilled her, as always, and she was very careful not to give herself over to him completely. There were rare occasions when she did that, but they usually took place in bed, and she usually hated herself afterward.

But she never hated him.

She broke the kiss and pushed away from him, saying, "Well, have a good trip and for Christ's sake, be careful. I don't want to get any telegrams calling for me to come and save you."

She was referring to the time *she* had sent *him* a telegram from Oklahoma saying that exact thing.*

"I'll watch myself," he promised.

Much of his trip from San Francisco to Texas had taken place by rail, but he preferred to ride into Huntsville himself so as not to bring any special attention to his arrival. He had loaded his dapple gray, Two-Pair, into the train in San Francisco, and the final leg of the trip to Huntsville served to exercise the animal sufficiently after the long train ride.

Now, with his arrival in Huntsville, he put San Francisco—and the people—behind him and adjusted his mind to the work ahead. When he was on a job, Tracker was all business, and with the payoff that lay ahead of him—in the event of success—he was determined to be even more businesslike than usual.

---

*Tracker #5: *The Oklahoma Score.*

[6]

Upon arriving in Huntsville Tracker put his horse up at one of the town's livery stables and registered at the Huntsville Hotel. The town itself was not particularly large, and much of its revenue came from the nearby Huntsville Prison.

William Jeffery had explained that while there was now in existence a written agreement between Tracker and the Bank of Huntsville, the bank would prefer that his employment did not become public knowledge. For this reason Tracker couldn't earn the right to ask questions by explaining that he was working for the bank. What he decided to do was just ask questions, and let people think he was simply out for the reward.

Of course, the first place he had to go for answers was the bank itself, where instructions had been left for everyone to cooperate fully with him, but he decided to stop at a nearby saloon first and see what he could pick up just by keeping his ears open for a while.

A half hour after Tracker had arrived in town, Heck Thomas knew about it. He had spread around a combination of money and fear to make sure that it wouldn't take much longer than that. Thomas didn't want to waste any time in sizing up his opposition, and when Tracker entered the Pretty Lady Saloon, Thomas was watching. When the big man stayed inside for longer than it would have normally taken for one dust-clearing drink, the detective decided to go in and take a closer look.

Tracker had finished one quick dust-clearing drink, then ordered a second and took it to a back table with

25

him. The saloon was not particularly large and, unless one contrived to keep one's voice down, a good listener could pretty much pick up any conversation.

Tracker was a damned good listener.

He was also a gifted observer. At times he found himself noticing things that on the surface would seem inconsequential, and then later would turn out to be important. When the solid-looking man entered the saloon Tracker noticed that before he walked to the bar his eyes swept the room, not in the general way of someone taking in his surroundings, but like someone looking for someone in particular. When the man installed himself at the bar with a drink Tracker directed his attention to a table one removed from his, where two men, apparently prison guards, were talking.

"I sure would like to take some time off to go looking for that money myself," one man said.

"I'd settle for my goddamned salary," the other man said, sourly.

"That'll come soon enough."

"Yeah, well, I can't feed my family with big promises, and some of us can't afford to wait like you can, Willis."

"I just handle my money better than most," the man called Willis said.

"That may be, but if I don't get paid soon, I'm gonna have to go looking for a job somewhere else."

"If you walk out you won't get a job in any other prison, Simmons," Willis warned.

Simmons made a face and finished his drink.

"I'm getting out of here, Willis," he said, slamming his empty glass down. "I can't afford to have another drink."

"Hold on, I'll come with you," Willis said. "If you're talking about walking out, I wanna hear more."

There were several other occupied tables in the saloon, even though it was still pretty early, and much of the conversation Tracker overheard revolved around the bank robbery, but none really had anything specific to do with it. He decided that if he couldn't get any more than what he'd gotten from Willis and Simmons, then he wouldn't waste any more time. He got up to go over to the bank and actively start what William Jeffery would call his "investigation."

On his way to the door he noticed—again, more subconsciously than otherwise—that the man at the bar seemed to follow his progress with interest. He filed the man away in his memory so that he'd be sure to recognize him if he saw him again.

And he had the feeling that he would.

[7]

The Bank of Huntsville was an impressive setup. It was easily the largest bank Tracker had ever seen outside of San Francisco. Tracker bypassed the row of teller's cages and walked to the first of several desks.

There was a young lady seated at that desk and when she looked up at the man standing before her, her eyes widened behind wire rim spectacles. He was easily the largest, most imposing figure she had ever seen.

Tracker thought that the girl's eyes looked particularly soft and wondered if it was because of the specs. They were gray, like his, but not flint gray. Instead, they were a hazy color which made them look very gentle. She had brown hair pulled back into a bun, small but pleasant features, and was wearing a high-necked dress. As he stared down at her, her hand rose and rested against the base of her throat.

"C-can I help you?"

"I'd like to see the bank president, please."

The girl swallowed and said, "M-may I tell him what it's in reference to?"

"Yes. A rather large, unscheduled withdrawal from your bank."

"A with—I-I don't think I understand."

"That's all right," Tracker assured her, "he'll understand."

She hesitated a moment, then started as if she realized that she should be getting up and bringing his message to the bank president.

"I'll be just a moment."

He watched her walk to the rear of the bank, enjoying the way her slim backside moved beneath her long dress. She disappeared through a door after knocking

28

gently, then reappeared just moments later and returned to where Tracker was waiting.

"Mr. Griffin will see you now."

"Thank you."

"You may go right in."

He started past her and she was preparing to sit back down behind her desk when he turned and said, "Excuse me?"

She stopped short and stood up straight, looking back at him over her shoulder.

"Yes?"

"What's your name?"

"Oh, my name is Norine. Norine Castle."

He smiled down at her and said, "My name is Tracker, Norine, and thank you for your help."

"I was . . . just doing my job," she said, looking somewhat bewildered.

"And very well, I might add."

"Thank you."

When he turned and walked toward the door to the president's office, he was sure that she was still standing watching him.

He knocked briefly on the door and entered.

"Mr. Tracker?" the man behind the desk asked. He was not particularly tall, somewhat portly, with a mane of wild gray hair, gray muttonchops and a gray mustache.

"That's right."

"I'm Warner Griffin, sir," the man said, coming around the desk with his right hand stuck out before him. "President of the Bank of Huntsville."

Tracker accepted the hand, found it a distasteful experience, shook it abruptly and released it. The man had a weak, damp grip and it had a definite effect on Tracker's opinion of him.

"Any way I can help you, sir," the man babbled, "any way at all, please don't hesitate to ask."

"Thank you."

"Please, have a seat."

Griffin hurried around behind his desk and sat down while Tracker seated himself in a visitor's chair.

"You can start by answering a question for me," Tracker said to the man.

"Of course."

"William Jeffery."

"What about him?" Griffin asked, frowning.

"Well, he has credentials that identify him as an 'officer of the Bank of Huntsville, Texas.' I find that ... unusual."

"What is unusual about it?"

"He's not President, he's not Vice-President. Just what is he?"

"Just what his credentials say he is. An officer of the bank." Griffin realized that the answer did not satisfy the big man and added, "You see, Mr. Jeffery's father founded this bank, and when he passed away he stipulated that his son should maintain a position at the bank, although not a position of, ah, great authority."

"Not the man his father was, is that it?"

"Well, not when it comes to banking. William is sort of our unofficial Chairman of the Board."

"And it was his idea to bring me in?"

"Yes, but the Board agreed to the move. We will do whatever we can to recover that money, Mr. Tracker—"

"Just call me Tracker."

"Yes, uh, Tracker. We would really like to be able to say that we recovered the money ourselves. It would go a long way toward restoring the faith our depositors had in us."

"I understand. Mr. Griffin, do you know a man named Bishop?"

"Bishop? What's his first name?"

That question annoyed Tracker because he had never bothered to find out Bishop's full name.

"Bishop is all I know," Tracker said quickly and then went on to describe the man.

Griffin listened intently and then shook his head and said, "I'm sorry, I don't know the man. Is it important?"

"Not very," Tracker said, dismissing the matter. "What can you tell me, Mr. Griffin, that Mr. Jeffery couldn't?"

"Well, there are several points that William was not aware of when we sent—uh, when we let him go to San Francisco to talk to you. Actually, we didn't want him telling you *too* much more than was necessary because, uh ..."

30

"Because you figured I might not take the job and go after the money myself."

"Well, you must understand we only knew of you by reputation—"

"That's not true."

"I beg your pardon?"

"I tend to keep a low profile, Mr. Griffin. You wouldn't have heard of me unless you knew the right people, and you'll pardon me if I say that you don't appear to be the sort of man who would know those sort of people."

"Well, one of our Board members knows certain people in Washington and heard that you had performed a service for, uh, President Garfield..."*

"All right," Tracker said, rescuing the uncomfortable Mr. Griffin, "I understand. Let's get to the pertinent facts."

"Very well," the bank president said. "The most pertinent fact of all is that one of our tellers was involved with the bank robbery."

"One of your people? If you know that, what's the problem? Finding him?"

"We know where he is, and we've sent people to talk to him, but we haven't been able to get any information out of him. To be frank, I don't think we've been able to, uh, talk to him the way he should be talked to."

Tracker frowned, wondering what the catch was. Why did they need him?

"How long was the man working here?"

"Just a few months. Long enough to know just when we'd have the payroll in addition to the rest of the money."

"So he bided his time and then let the others know when the bank was overloaded, huh?"

"That's what we think."

"Explain the robbery to me."

"It was fairly straightforward. Four masked men entered the bank, brandished their guns and proceeded to clean us out. One of our other tellers noticed that

---

*Tracker #3: *The Blue Cut Job*.

Barlow—the teller involved—seemed to know the robbers. After the robbery the sheriff called him on it and he broke down. I'm afraid he wasn't very strong."

"Which is probably why he was chosen to be the inside man. If he folded under the pressure, then why haven't you been able to get him to talk further?"

Griffin shrugged.

"Perhaps he's discovered some steel in his backbone due to his present surroundings."

"Well, I guess I'd better start out by having a talk with him," Tracker said, standing. "Just tell me where to find him."

"He'll be very easy to find, Tracker," Griffin said. "He is an inmate in the Huntsville Penitentiary."

Before leaving Griffin's office Tracker asked the man how many people had been instructed to cooperate with him. The bank president told him that all of the officers, "and my personal secretary, Miss Castle," had received those instructions.

Upon leaving the man's office Tracker stopped once again at Norine Castle's desk. Startled, she looked up.

"Yes?"

Tracker leaned over so that only she would be able to hear him.

"I understand that you've been told to cooperate with me fully."

"Yes, that's right."

"Good. I think I might have some questions that you will be able to answer for me."

"I don't know what I could tell—"

"Ah-ah, Miss Castle, you'll have to let me be the judge of that," Tracker said, wiggling his forefinger.

"Very well," she said, squaring her shoulders. "Ask your questions. I will do my best to answer them."

"I appreciate your willingness to help, but at the moment I've got to go and question a man in prison."

"Really?" she asked, her eyes widening.

"Yes, so I'm afraid I'll have to ask you those questions later . . . over dinner."

"Dinner? I don't—"

"It will be bank business, Miss Castle," he said, hurriedly, "I assure you."

"Well—"

"You could be a very big help to me," he said, sensing that she was weakening.

"Well," she said, "if it's for the good of the bank—"

"Oh, it is."

She leaned forward a bit, saying in a conspiratorial whisper, "Could I really be a help to you in—you know, recovering...the money?" The last word was almost totally inaudible.

Tracker, lowering his voice and leaning further over her desk, said, "Invaluable."

"Very well, then," she said, "for the good of the bank I shall have dinner with you."

"Am I that hard to take?" Tracker asked, straightening up abruptly.

"Oh, I certainly didn't mean *that*, Mr. Tracker, I assure you," she informed him hurriedly. "As a matter of fact, I think you're *very* attractive." She seemed to realize what she had said a split second too late, and her face colored as her hands flew to her mouth.

"Thank you, Miss Castle," Tracker said. "You don't know what this will mean to me."

"And to the bank," she reminded him.

"Yes, of course," he agreed, "the bank."

She told Tracker where she lived—above the general store—and they agreed that he would pick her up at seven o'clock.

Tracker left the bank, wondering just what it was about Norine Castle that drove him to such a deception.

From his vantage point across the street from the bank, Heck Thomas stared after Tracker, walking away from the building, absently rubbed his jaw, then started after him.

[8]

Tracker had no problem getting into the Huntsville Penitentiary to see the imprisoned teller, Jesse Barlow. Apparently, someone had spoken to the warden—possibly from Washington again? Tracker had certainly never expected the Blue Cut job to result in some references from Washington, but then why not? He'd done a hell of a job.

A uniformed guard brought Barlow to a small room and left Tracker alone with him after relieving him of his gun.

Barlow the teller was a thin wisp of a man, barely five and a half feet tall who looked like he'd have a hard time standing up against a stiff breeze. His face was bruised in a couple of places, scraped in another, and when he moved it was like a man who's been hit in the ribs once too often. Tracker knew that prison couldn't be an easy place for a young man like Jesse Barlow, but there was something about the young man's eyes....

Something was happening to him in Huntsville Penitentiary aside from being beaten—probably by inmates and guards alike.

He was getting stronger.

"How old are you?"

That surprised Jesse Barlow. It might have been the last question he expected to hear.

"Twenty-two," he answered. "Who are you?"

"I'm the fella who's supposed to scare you into telling me where the money is."

"What money?"

"But that wouldn't work, Jesse, would it?"

"Not likely. It was tried already."

"By who?"

"Big detective fella."

"What'd he look like?"

"Big man with big hands, hadn't shaved in a while, not as lean as you..."

The picture of the man in the saloon came up from Tracker's subconscious, as he had known it would. He hadn't seen the man again, but here they were crossing paths.

"They tell me you folded up like an old deck of cards when the sheriff questioned you," Tracker said, getting back on the track.

The young man's face hardened and he said, "Won't happen again."

"I believe you," Tracker said, and he did. Jesse Barlow was downright embarrassed about breaking down under the sheriff's questioning, and it was that embarrassment that would make him die before he'd do it again.

"So what are you gonna do?" Barlow asked, "try to beat it out of me?"

"I don't think so," Tracker said, looking Barlow straight in the eye. "I think if I hit you once I'd kill you."

The young man's jaw stiffened and he said belligerently, "Go ahead and try it."

"I don't think so. I think I'll offer you a deal, instead."

Barlow frowned and said, "What kind of deal?"

"How do you like it in Huntsville?"

"What the hell kind of question is that?"

"Just answer it."

Barlow hesitated, then said, "I hate it!"

"Do you know where the money is, Jesse?"

"I might."

"How would you know?"

"Because I know the boys who stole it, and I know where they'd hole up."

"How do you know that?"

Jesse Barlow looked proud when he answered, "Because they're my brothers."

"All of them?"

"All four," Barlow said, nodding.

"The Barlow brothers, huh?"

35

"That's right. We pulled off the biggest bank job in history. Bigger than anything the James boys ever pulled."

Tracker didn't have time to look it up, so he took the kid's word for it.

"I'll tell you what I want to do, Jesse," he said. "I'll get you out of here if you'll take me to your brothers."

"You must be crazy. I ain't takin' you and no posse to my brothers—"

"Did I say anything about a posse?" Tracker asked. "I'm not a lawman, Jesse. You take me to your brothers and I'll take that money off them myself."

"You think because you're big you'll be able to take the money away from them? You ain't even big enough to stand up to Jud."

"Who's Jud."

"My brother, Jud Barlow," Jesse Barlow said, leaning forward in his chair and warming to the subject. He was dressed in prison stripes and he was filthy, but there was such a look of great pride on his face when he talked about his brothers that Tracker didn't doubt he was telling the truth.

"Jud's the strongest man alive, and you think you can stand up to him *and* the others?"

"I say I can, Jesse," Tracker said. "I'll get you out of here and you can take me to them and let me prove it."

"They'll kill you the minute they lay eyes on you."

"That's a chance I'll take."

Tracker had been watching Jesse Barlow's eyes and finally saw what he was waiting for: the crafty gleam that said the boy was about to lie. Jesse finally realized that even though he might promise to help Tracker, he didn't have to keep his word once he was on the outside.

"All right," Jesse said.

"All right . . . what?"

"You got a deal."

"Say it, Jesse."

"If you get me out of here I'll take you to my brothers and they'll kill you dead."

Tracker grinned and said, "You got a deal, kid."

[9]

"Goddamnit—" Tracker exploded, but he was in his hotel room and there was nobody there to hear him.

After leaving Jesse Barlow in the hands of the guard who delivered him, Tracker went to see the warden of Huntsville Prison about getting Barlow released in his custody.

Warden John Stevens steadfastly refused to do so on the grounds that Tracker was not an officer of the law.

"I'll talk to the governor," Tracker said.

"You do that," Stevens replied. "Have him make you a U.S. Marshal, or even a deputy sheriff, and while you're at it have him order me to release the prisoner in your custody, because that's the only way I'm going to do it."

Tracker had stared coldly at Warden Stevens, but refused to allow the man to see how annoyed he was. He waited until he was in his hotel room to explode.

He didn't have time to fool around trying to get to see the governor and convincing him to go along with his plan. He was going to have to think of something else.

It was almost seven, so he undressed, washed up and then dressed in fresh clothes to pick up Norine Castle for dinner. Maybe while relaxing with her something would come to him.

Norine Castle looked quite different when Tracker met her at her rooms later. Her hair, worn in a tight bun that afternoon, was now falling softly about her shoulders. She had added some rouge to her cheeks and some color to her lips...and then there were those glasses.

Or rather, where were those glasses?

"I'm leaving the glasses behind," she said as they left to have dinner. She'd noticed him studying her closely, as if trying to figure out what was different.

"I noticed," he said. "You look lovely."

"Thank you, Mr.—"

"Call me Tracker."

"Don't you have a first name?"

"Yes."

"You won't tell me?"

"No."

"Maybe . . . later?" she asked.

"Maybe."

She was wearing a high-necked dress again, but this one allowed him to admire her slim body with its trim waist and small, well-rounded breasts.

Dinner was a pleasant affair and Tracker made sure they had lots of wine with it. The wine helped her get over whatever shyness would have been in their way. When he suggested that they go back to his room for a nightcap, she agreed.

When they got to his room the nightcap was forgotten as they helped each other out of their clothing without talking.

When he touched her bare breasts she shivered and when he lowered her to the bed and began to bite the nipples of her small, soft breasts, she moaned happily and ran her fingers through his hair. She could feel his cock, rigid and pulsing, trapped between them and she reached down to take it in her hand and guide it home. He entered her effortlessly and penetrated to the hilt, enjoying the burning hot wetness of her. He took her slim, almost boyish buttocks in his hands and dictated the pace of their thrusts so as to make the pleasure last as long as possible for both of them. He knew a lot of men who only thought of their own pleasure, and he was like that at times, but other times he liked to make sure that his partner enjoyed the coupling just as much as he did.

He could feel Norine Castle responding beneath him, her insides grabbing at him, milking him, and when he knew that she was on the brink of orgasm he hurried to join her so that they exploded together.

"Oh God," she said, "when I saw you, I knew..." and then she let it trail off.

"Knew what?" he asked her.

She smiled up at him, her hair fanned out on the pillow behind her, and said, "I just knew."

[10]

With Norine Castle asleep in his bed, Tracker left the hotel, heading for the nearest saloon. As he did so, he felt someone's presence behind him and when he turned to look, saw the man from the saloon again, the man Jesse Barlow had described.

"Can I buy you a drink?" he called out.

The man stepped off the boardwalk, out from the shadows where he'd been partially hidden, into the light from the street lamps.

"Why not?" the man replied. "Following you can get to be thirsty work."

"Heck Thomas," the other man introduced himself, once they were seated in the saloon with a beer before each of them.

"Tracker."

"I know."

"Then tell me something I don't know," Tracker said. "You've told me your name, now tell me who you are."

Heck Thomas introduced himself further as chief agent of the Texas Express Co.

"Now you're gonna ask me why the Texas Express Co. is interested in the Huntsville holdup."

"Not necessarily," Tracker said. "You can't be that highly paid that the reward doesn't appeal to you."

"Fine," Thomas said. "Why don't we just let it go at that?"

"So we're working against each other, then."

"I suppose."

"That's why you've been following me."

"All day."

Tracker didn't know whether to believe the man or

40

not. If he *had* been following him all day, then he was damned good at it.

"I've just been trying to figure out your style, that's all."

"Well, it hasn't been much more successful than yours, up to now."

They paused while Heck Thomas went to the bar to get two fresh beers.

When he returned he asked, "How'd your talk with Jesse Barlow go?"

"Not much better than yours, although I didn't threaten him, or hit him."

"I didn't lay a finger on him," Thomas said. "He got all those marks from the inmates—and the guards, more likely as not."

"That's what I figured. I did make a deal with Barlow, but the warden wouldn't go for it."

"What kind of deal?"

Tracker explained the agreement he and Barlow had come to.

"You didn't really believe him, did you? That he was going to lead you to his brothers?"

"Of course not. He'd have tried to get away first chance he got, and I'd have let him."

"And then followed him."

Tracker nodded and said, "Can't go through with it, though, unless I can get him out of there."

"What have you got in mind, Tracker?"

"Let me get another couple of beers and I'll tell you," Tracker said.

As he waited for the bartender to draw the fresh beers he wondered if maybe he and Heck Thomas shouldn't work together on this thing instead of against each other.

"I'll tell you what I've got in mind, Thomas, but first we've got to come to some sort of agreement," Tracker said as he set the beer in front of Thomas.

"What do you suggest?"

"That we work together instead of against each other."

"And split the reward?"

Tracker decided he wouldn't tell Thomas that he was collecting a fee and said, "Yeah, and split the reward."

Thomas studied Tracker and decided that he'd be

41

more than a worthy adversary. If they were busy butting heads, neither one of them would find the money.

"All right, Tracker," Thomas said, lifting his beer mug. "You've got a deal."

They touched mugs, drank and lowered them.

"Now, what have you got in mind?"

"Nothing too difficult," Tracker said. "You and me are gonna break Jesse Barlow out of the Huntsville Penitentiary."

[11]

"Do you really think this guy's deal is for real?" Jesse Barlow's cellmate asked.

"Who knows?" Barlow asked. "Who cares? As soon as he gets me out of here, I'm gone, John."

"Well, I wish you luck."

"Hey," Barlow said, struck by an idea, "maybe I can get him to take you, too."

"I doubt that," the other man said, laughing.

"Hey, you been pretty good to me since I been here. I'd like to pay you back."

"Really?"

"Sure."

The man named John studied the kid for a while, then sat up on his bunk and said, "Maybe there is a way you could pay me back."

"You're crazy!"

"Let me get you another beer," Tracker offered, and left Heck to think about it for a few moments.

When he came back he placed the fresh beer in front of the detective and said, "What do you think?"

Heck sipped his beer, looked Tracker in the eye and then repeated, "You're crazy."

"Look, it's not so crazy," Tracker said, leaning forward. "We break him without hurting anybody, use him to get the money back and catch his brothers and then bring them all back. It's simple."

"It's against the law."

"Nobody will ever know it was us who broke him

out," Tracker explained, "but we'll sure as hell get all the credit for bringing them back—with the money."

Heck Thomas wasn't convinced.

"We'll get all the credit—and the reward."

Heck Thomas was convinced.

[12]

When Tracker returned to his hotel room feeling the effects of all the drinks he'd shared with Heck Thomas, Norine Castle was still curled up in his bed, asleep.

As he undressed he again went over his proposal to Heck Thomas in his own mind, and found it sound. Sliding into bed next to Norine, he wondered if it would be as sound in the cold light of day, when his head was totally clear.

Norine moaned and rolled toward him, placing one hand against his chest and the other on his crotch. As her fingers moved he swelled to fill her hand and, wordlessly, she slid atop him. He placed his hands on her smooth flanks and eased himself into her. Her hips began to move insistently and he decided to let her go at her own speed, this time.

The speed of her thrusts against him increased and soon she was breathing shortly in his ear, her breath coming in guttural rasps.

"Oh God—" she whispered at one point, and she knew she was about to come. He relaxed and as her tremors began he began to fill her up.

"You went away," she said in a small voice, her mouth at the hollow of his neck.

"Not for very long."

"Where did you go?"

What was he to tell her?

"I had to go and see a man about a jailbreak."

"That's nice," she said, and went back to sleep.

[13]

The next morning Tracker headed for a breakfast meeting with Heck Thomas, while Norine Castle went to the bank for her day's work. Tracker agreed to meet her later, but secretly hoped to be gone from Huntsville by that time. He'd make it up to her when he came back.

He found the small cafe Heck had told him about and the detective was there waiting for him.

"I ordered coffee."

"That's good enough for me," Tracker said, sitting across from the man.

"Hell, if I knew you weren't gonna eat I'd've ordered for myself."

"Be my guest."

When the waitress came with the coffee Heck ordered a breakfast of steak, eggs, ham, potatoes, and biscuits.

"You going to eat all that?" Tracker asked, pouring himself a cup of coffee.

"I always get hungry when I'm about to break someone out of jail."

"Then you agree?"

Heck made a face but said, "Yeah, I agree. I can't see any way around it."

"Well," Tracker said with satisfaction, "I think I might have a little breakfast myself. Once we're on the run, who knows when we'll eat well again?"

"Don't remind me."

Over breakfast they discussed how they would go about breaking Jesse Barlow out of jail.

"Have you ever done this before?" Heck asked.

Tracker paused a moment, then said, "Not from the outside."

Heck frowned, but decided not to pursue the remark. He was afraid of what he might find out.

"What's the best way to do this, then?"

"Well, since I've got experience doing it from the inside," Tracker said, "why don't we do it that way?"

"From the inside?"

"Sure."

"How?"

"Just walk right in and take him out."

"Just like that."

"Yeah, just like that."

"I think maybe you'd better explain this to me," Heck said. "My style would be to blast out a wall or something."

"That might work," Tracker said, "but I think my way is better. He's not in maximum security, so it shouldn't be that difficult. Listen..."

When Tracker asked the warden if he could see Jesse Barlow again, the man agreed. Tracker thought the man might be trying to make up for not cooperating the day before. If that was the case, the warden was going to end up a mighty disappointed man—and a slightly foolish one.

Tracker had convinced Heck Thomas not to come into the prison with him. As many ways as he tried to figure the escape, there was practically no way they *weren't* going to be looking for Tracker after the break, so he figured why should the law be looking for both of them. Heck agreed, then, to do the outside work— stocking up on supplies and buying the horses—while Tracker went in to get Barlow.

"You'll be a wanted man after this, you know," Heck reminded him.

"Only until we bring the money back," Tracker said. "The bank will take care of it after that."

"For your sake," Heck Thomas said, "I hope so."

A guard brought Barlow to the same room where they'd spoken the day before, took Tracker's gun, and left them alone.

"What about our deal?" Barlow asked immediately.

"Our deal still stands," Tracker said, assuring him,

47

"but we're going to have to go about it a little differently."

Barlow frowned and asked, "What do you mean?"

"The warden wouldn't go along with our deal—"

"Then the deal is off!"

"Cool off," Tracker said. "I said the *warden* wouldn't go along with it. I'm still willing."

"Oh, yeah? What are you gonna do," Barlow demanded, "break me out?"

"Yes."

Barlow stared at Tracker for a few moments and then said, "You're serious."

"Yes, I am. Are you?"

"About what?"

"About wanting to get out of here."

"Hell, yes!"

"Just remember one thing," Tracker said. "If you try anything funny I'll bring you right back here."

Barlow grinned and said, "How you gonna do that if you're dead? My brothers *are* gonna kill you, you know."

"Well, if I don't get you out of here they're never going to get the chance, so let's work on that for now."

"Did you bring me a gun?"

Tracker reached into the waist of his pants, behind his belt, and brought out a little two-shot derringer that Heck Thomas had supplied.

"Good. Give it to me."

"Uh-uh," Tracker said, shaking his head. "I handle the guns, friend. You just come along for the ride."

"Come on, come on, give me the gun!"

"We'll do this my way or we won't do it at all, kid," Tracker said. "Make your choice."

"Damn!" Barlow hissed. "All right, let's go."

"I'm going to call for the guard. Stand away from the door."

Barlow obeyed and Tracker moved to the door and called out. He stepped aside and as the door opened and the guard started in he jammed the barrel of the little derringer into the side of the man's neck.

"Take it easy."

"Hey—"

"Don't talk," Tracker said, taking his gun back from

48

the man. He tucked away the derringer and palmed his own gun, then relieved the guard of his gun and tucked it into his belt.

"Sorry, friend, but you're in the middle of this," Tracker said, and brought the barrel of his gun down on the back of the man's head.

"Now you can give me a gun," Barlow insisted, rushing forward.

"Back off!" Tracker commanded, pointing his gun at Barlow.

"We have a better chance if you give me a gun."

"You have a better chance of shooting me in the back, you mean. No, kid, we're still doing this my way."

"Okay," Barlow said, putting his hands on his hips, "what now?"

"Now we're going out the back way."

"Good," Barlow said, "we have to pass my cell to go out the back way and I have to pick something up." He leaned over and took the keys from the guard.

"Let's go," Tracker said impatiently. "Lead the way."

Barlow left the room first and started down the hall.

"What are we gonna do if we run into a guard?" he asked. "You ain't gonna kill him, are you?"

"No."

"Then what?"

"Whoever we run into won't know that I won't kill him," Tracker said. "Just keep going. I'm sure you know how to avoid a guard."

"Yeah, that's one of the first things you learn in here."

They went on a little further and then Barlow said, "I'm not in maximum security, so we just might be able to make it without running into anybody."

"Keep going."

They reached Barlow's block of cells and Tracker couldn't help thinking that it had been too easy up to this point. Something had to go wrong.

"Wait," Barlow said as they reached his cell. "This one's mine."

"What is it you want to pick up?"

There was a man in the cell, lying on a bunk, and as he sat up Barlow pointed to him and said, "Him!"

[14]

"You're nuts!" Tracker said.

"He's my friend, Tracker," Barlow said. "If he don't go, I don't go."

"Hey, kid—" the man in the cell started.

"Easy, John," Barlow said, holding his hand out to the man. "I've got to do this."

"Barlow, they could be after us any minute," Tracker said. "Are you coming?"

"Not without him."

Tracker actually believed the kid was serious. He looked at the man in the cell, who shrugged at him helplessly, as if to say he had nothing to do with it.

"Jesus," Tracker said. "All right, goddamnit, let him out, and hurry."

Barlow took out the keys he'd gotten off the guard, fumbled with them for a few seconds before getting the right key in the lock. He swung the cell door open and threw the keys inside.

"Let's go, John."

"I'm with you, Jesse," John said, stepping out of the cell, "and, uh, your friend, here."

"Friend," Tracker said in disgust. "Let's go, Barlow."

"This way."

They started down the hall toward the end and suddenly the other inmates began to make noise, shouting and yelling to be let out.

"Swell," Tracker said, under his breath. "Come on, move," he told the two men ahead of him, "move your asses."

As they reached the end of the hall the door opened and a guard stepped into the hall. When he saw the three men heading toward him he grabbed for his sidearm. For a moment Tracker thought that the only way they'd get out would be for him to shoot the man, but John moved quickly, racing ahead of Barlow and hitting the man on the butt of the jaw with his fist. The guard went down and John bent over to retrieve his gun. When he straightened up he was looking down the barrel of Tracker's gun.

"Hand it over," Tracker said.

They traded stares for a few seconds and then John shrugged, smiled and handed over the gun.

"Whatever you say, friend."

Tracker tucked the gun into his belt with the other guard's and said, "Now, let's move."

As they did they heard a horn sound and knew that the alarm had been given.

"This way!" John shouted, taking the lead.

He led the way to the rear of the prison and when they broke through the door to the outside the guards on the wall began firing.

"Where to?" Barlow asked, looking panicky.

"There!" Tracker replied, pointing straight ahead. There was a small rise and then a dip and that was where Heck Thomas was supposed to be waiting with the horses.

They ran in that direction with chunks of lead gouging out pieces of the ground behind them.

"Here!" Heck Thomas shouted as they crested the rise, and they saw the detective standing with three horses.

"There are only three horses," Jesse Barlow complained.

"There were only supposed to be three of us," Tracker reminded him.

"Well, who's that guy?" Barlow demanded, and then he recognized Heck. "Hey, wait a minute—"

The guards on the wall were starting to get the range and hot lead began landing dangerously close to them.

"You want to argue or get the hell out of here?" Tracker asked.

"Jesse," John said, "let's get the hell out of here and argue later."

"Yeah, okay," Barlow said.

51

"You two ride double," Tracker said. He took Two-Pair's reins from Heck and mounted up. "Let's go."

The others mounted and spurred their horses on as guards began to pour from the back of the prison. Tracker felt something tug at his shirt sleeve, but did not stop to see what it was. They rode on, spreading out so as to make more difficult targets, and rode until the prison was far behind them.

"Which way?" Tracker asked Heck.

"Follow me."

Heck led the way to where he had cached a pack horse carrying a light load. A full load would only have slowed them down.

"When we get some distance between us and Huntsville we'll divvy up the supplies and cut the packhorse loose," Tracker had explained earlier.

"All right," Tracker said as Heck gathered in the other animal's reins, "let's ride."

"I don't think we'll all make it," a voice said from behind the two of them.

They turned and saw that the speaker was the man called John. He was riding in front of Jesse Barlow, and as they watched, Barlow slid off the back of the horse and fell to the ground.

"Christ," Heck Thomas said.

He had fallen on his face and they could all see the hole in his back. Tracker dismounted and rushed over to him, but he already knew that it was too late.

"He's dead."

"That's fine," Heck Thomas said in disgust. "That's just great. What the hell do we do now?"

Tracker stood over the body of the dead man and said, "Heck, you better get out of here."

"What are you going to do?"

"I'll bring this fella back to the prison and try to explain things to the warden."

"He'll throw you in Barlow's cell."

"I don't think so," Tracker said, recalling how easy the escape had been up to a point. "I don't really think so."

"Excuse me," the other man said, "but can I say something?"

"You can say whatever you like, mister, but you're going back," Tracker said.

"I don't think so."

"What makes you say that?" Heck Thomas asked.

"Well, see, I know that you were breaking the kid so that he could take you to his brothers and the bank's money."

"No chance of that now," Heck said.

"No, actually there is," the man said, disagreeing.

"Mister, if you've got something to say you'd best get to it," Tracker said.

"Fine with me," John said. "I know where the money is—or at least, I know where Jesse thought it and his brothers were."

"And just how do you know that?" Heck asked.

John gestured to the dead man and said, "He told me."

"Why would he do a fool thing like that?" Heck asked.

"I sort of took him under my wing when he got to the prison," John said. "You know, kept him from getting beat up even worse than he did?"

"And for that he told you where the money was?" Heck asked, looking at the man dubiously.

"He said he wished there was some way to thank me," the man said, spreading his hands in a helpless gesture.

Heck made a disgusted noise and said, "I don't believe a word of it." He looked at Tracker and said, "He just doesn't want to go back, that's all."

Tracker had been studying the man for the past few moments and came to a decision.

"I don't think we can take the chance, Heck." Looking at the detective he said, "We can't afford not to believe him."

"There you go," John said. Addressing himself directly to Heck Thomas he added, "Shall we get started? They're bound to be after us by now."

"Tracker—" Heck started, warningly.

"What have we got to lose, Heck?"

"Only our freedom," the detective said, "and maybe our lives."

Tracker shrugged and said, "Then let's ride."

* * *

Tracker and Heck decided that they didn't have time to bury Jesse Barlow.

"Besides," Tracker offered, "they'll have to stop and bury him and that'll slow them down some."

With that they rode off, leaving the body of Jesse Barlow behind. It never entered Tracker or Heck Thomas's head to feel guilt over the young man's death. He had brought the entire situation on himself—he and his brothers.

Tracker admitted to himself that the other man, John, might have been lying—and probably was—but just on the off chance that Barlow had talked to his cellmate, they had to take the chance.

Hell, it was the only one they had.

[15]

They camped that night in a gulley, refraining from building a fire, and dined on cold beef jerky.

"Even this is better than what we got in Huntsville," John commented.

"What do we call you besides 'John'?" Tracker asked him then.

"John will do," the man replied, reaching for another slice of jerky.

"You ashamed of who you are?" Heck Thomas asked.

"No," John replied, "I just don't want to clutter up our relationship with unnecessary facts."

Tracker and Heck exchanged glances and Tracker shrugged. What was the difference, anyway?

"You want to tell us where you're taking us?" he asked.

"No."

"What do you mean, no?" Heck demanded.

"If I tell you where we're going," John said, "you won't need me anymore, will you?"

Neither man had an answer for him.

"That's what I thought," their guide said. "If I give you the location, I'm right back in the pen."

"I still don't believe you," Heck Thomas said, "and if I find out I'm right, you're gonna wish you were back in the Huntsville pen."

"I'll tell you again," John said, patiently. "Jesse was grateful to me for taking him under my wing. He was new blood in Huntsville, if you know what I mean. I helped him out and he wanted to show his gratitude."

"And you did it out of the goodness of your heart, right?" Heck asked.

"I did it," John said seriously, "because he was my

cellmate. That's something you'd probably never understand." John looked over at Tracker and added, "You probably would, though, wouldn't you?"

"Just make sure you do what you say you can do, *John*," Tracker said.

"Don't worry," the man said in reassuring tones, "I'll take you to the Barlow boys *and* the money. After that, the rest is up to you gents. Now, if you don't mind, I think I'll get some shuteye. You fellas can split the watch."

Heck bit back a sharp remark and fumed silently while the man made himself comfortable.

"I'll take the first watch," Tracker said. "In the morning we'll divvy up the supplies. He'll carry his share, so we don't overload ourselves."

"Fine," Heck said, still staring at the motionless man. "If it turns out he's lying—"

"No sense worrying about it, Heck," Tracker said. "It's the only way we've got to go, right now, so let's be as positive as we can be in our thinking."

"Sure," Heck said, under his breath, "if he's lying, I'm *positive* I'm gonna kill him."

[16]

The next day they rose early and rode all morning and afternoon, pausing to rest the horses once. During that rest period Tracker suggested that Heck ride back behind them and see how close—if indeed they were close at all—their pursuers were.

"Where will we meet?" Heck asked.

"In a town called Lorenville, just this side of the Mexican border."

"Who says we're going to Mexico?" John asked.

"Who says we're not?" Tracker replied. "All I'm saying is that we'll meet there. Where we go from there will be up to you."

"Jesus," Heck said.

"You're taking a big chance, Heck," John said, giving Heck an amused look. "What makes you think Tracker is really gonna meet you in Lorenville? If he does that, he'll have to share the money with you when we find it."

"I'll tell you what, sonny," Heck said, pointing his index finger. "I trust him a hell of a lot more than I trust you. Besides, he knows that if he tries to cheat me I'll find him and one of us will end up dead."

"That's for sure," Tracker said. "Go ahead, Heck. We'll meet in Lorenville."

"Right."

"You don't have any sentimental attachment to that horse, do you?"

"Why would I have those kind of feelings about something I might have to eat someday?"

Tracker didn't know if he could ever get hungry enough to eat Two-Pair, but he said, "All right. That means you can ride him as hard as you like to catch up with us because we'll get you another in Lorenville."

"Right. See you there."

As Heck rode off John looked at Tracker and asked, "Are you really gonna meet him in that town?"

"You bet."

"Why?"

"Because the last thing I want to do is try to kill that man," Tracker said, "and just for your information, I don't feel the same way about you. Let's go."

As Heck Thomas retraced their trail he thought over what the convict, John, had said, but then decided that taking anything seriously that John said was foolish—and wasn't that what they were being already? Heck was content to let Tracker call the play, because the break had been his idea and his butt was on the line if it didn't work, but he was only going to go along with the big man so far. If it turned out that "John" was stringing them along, looking for a chance to break free, he was going to take matters into his own hands.

When Heck topped a rise he pulled back on his horse hard and eased behind a stand of brush. From there he could see a posse of about twelve men, but the funny thing about it was that they were standing still. There were two men at the front and they were deep in conversation. Heck wished he could hear what was being said.

"What do you think?" the first of those two men asked. "Should we go a little further?"

"I don't think so," the second man said. "The warden just said to make it look good. I think we can turn back now."

"What do you think the warden has in mind?"

"I don't know," the other man said. "Maybe he's looking to get our money back. He ain't been paid either, you know."

"Don't remind me," the first man said, and signaled the unofficial posse to turn back.

Heck frowned when the posse turned back, then wheeled his horse around and urged him into an all-out run. Why the posse had given up the chase he didn't know—but he had an idea, and he wanted to check it out with Tracker.

Outside Lorenville John called Tracker to a sudden halt.

"What's wrong?"

"I can't go into town looking like this," the man said, indicating his prison clothing. "I wouldn't make a very good first impression on people, and we'd attract much too much attention."

As much as he hated to, Tracker had to admit that the man had a point.

"All right," Tracker said, dismounting and reaching into his saddlebag, "I'll give you a shirt, but you'll have to keep those pants on. When we get to town I'll buy you a change of clothes."

"That's mighty nice of you."

"Yeah," Tracker said. He threw John a shirt and said, "Try that one on."

The shirt's sleeves hung over John's hands; he had to fold the cuffs up over his wrists.

"Leave the tail out," Tracker instructed him. "It'll hide some of those prison pants."

"If you gave me a pair of pants they'd come up to my chest."

"Not hardly," Tracker said, "but I ain't giving you a pair of pants, so get that thought out of your mind."

"I'd much rather you gave me a gun," John said. "When we catch up to the Barlow boys, you'll need an extra hand."

"I'll have one."

"I mean besides ol' Heck."

"Ol' Heck will do me just fine when the time comes."

"That's okay," John said confidently, "I can wait until you ask."

"Until I—" Tracker began, staring at the man. "Uh, listen John, you just do your part and take us to the Barlows, okay?"

"Sure, always ready to do my part," the convict said. "Wanna go to town now?"

"I think that's a good idea," Tracker said, mounting up. "Let's go to town."

[17]

When they got to town they put the horses up at the livery and tried to ignore the curious stares of the liveryman.

"Where to now?" John asked as they left the livery.

"I think we'd better get you that change of clothes first before we do anything else."

"Fine with me."

"I wasn't asking your opinion," Tracker said in annoyance. "Look, John-or-whatever-your-name-is, don't forget what your position is in all this. You're an escaped convict—"

"I know that," John broke in. "You helped me escape, remember?"

"I remember, and I can put you right back inside again. Don't forget that."

"Sure," John said, wearing that same look of amusement he'd been wearing all along, "we could even share a cell together."

"That's not going to happen, Johnny boy, so don't even think about it."

They reached a small store that sold men's clothing and went inside. Tracker bought John one shirt, one pair of pants, a pair of boots and a hat, all cheap. The convict changed into his new clothes immediately.

"You know," John said as they left the shop, "these are not exactly the clothes I would have picked out."

"If and when you ever get a chance to buy your own clothes with your own money again, you can buy whatever you want. Right now, those will have to do."

"Well, they're a lot better than those prisoner stripes I was wearing. What's the chances of getting a bath?"

"Let's get a hotel room first, and then we'll see about a bath."

They went over to the Lorenville Hotel and checked into one room. Tracker figured that Heck could check into his own room when he got there, but he wanted to make sure he always had his eye on John.

"You got bath facilities?" John asked the clerk.

"In the back, sir."

John gave Tracker a hopeful look and Tracker relented, saying, "All right. I guess I could use one, too. Let's put the gear in the room, first."

They dropped off the saddlebags from both their horses, along with Tracker's rifle, but as they were about to leave the room John brought up something that had been on his mind since the jailbreak.

"I need a woman."

"What?"

"I want a woman with my bath," John said. "I've been inside a long time, Tracker."

"You want me to pimp for you?" Tracker asked in disbelief.

"It's either that or you might as well take me back to Huntsville right now."

Tracker was about to grab John with both of his big hands and shake him up, but thought better of it. He could always do that later. Right now, the more he thought about it, the better a woman with the bath sounded.

"Let's go downstairs."

When they got to the lobby Tracker spoke to the clerk.

"I'd like to arrange for some female companion-ship—"

"Oh, sir, we couldn't—"

"...with the bath."

"I'm sorry," the man said, shaking his head, but his head stopped shaking when Tracker took out ten dollars and brushed it under the man's nose.

"How many girls?"

"Just one."

"Blonde," John said, "and plump."

"I think that can be arranged, sir," the man said. "Of

61

course you'll have to make your own, er, arrangement with the girl."

"No problem," Tracker said.

"Fine, fine. I'll take care of it, sir."

They walked to the bath facilities and, once in the room, Tracker said, "You go first. I'm going to keep a close eye on you so don't try anything funny with the soap."

"Soap? You're going to let me use soap? What are you going to do when it's your turn in the tub?"

"My gun is going to be right by me, friend, so don't think you can cross the room before I can reach it."

"I wouldn't dream of it. I'm sure you're a real capable fella."

John was undressed and in the tub when there was a knock on the door.

"Come in," Tracker called.

The door opened and a girl stuck her head in.

"Right here, sweetheart," John said, waving from the tub.

She looked at John, then at Tracker, and then entered the room slowly.

"Both of you?" she asked.

"Me, me," John said, waving again.

She frowned and looked at Tracker.

"Not you?" she asked, hoping that he'd say yes.

Tracker shrugged and said, "Take care of my friend, first, and then we'll see."

"Sure," she said, starting for the tub.

She had a rather plain face, but that didn't matter to John. She was blonde, had long hair, and was buxom with a plump behind. She shed her plain one-piece dress as she approached the tub.

From the front John could see that her breasts were big and firm, with pink nipples the size of his thumb tips. Between her rather plump thighs her furry patch was pale.

From behind Tracker examined her voluptuous, muscular buttocks. Dressed, she might have appeared to be a tad overweight, but stripped down he could see that it was all muscle. His dick started to harden and he crossed his legs.

"Hey, wait a minute," John said, looking past the girl at Tracker. "You're gonna watch?"

"I'm not letting you out of my sight." The girl looked at Tracker over her shoulder and he asked, "Do you mind, honey?"

"Hell, no."

Tracker looked at John and shrugged and the man in the tub said, "Okay, if that's the way it's got to be. Come here, girl."

She approached the tub and got down to her knees so that John could grasp her breasts.

"Ouch," she said. "You been without long, mister?"

"You don't know the half of it."

She helped him bathe, taking the soap and lathering his chest and back, and then worked her hands lower until his long, slim erection was in her hands.

"You got a skinny one," she said, massaging it up and down.

"Don't you worry how skinny it is, girl."

"My name's Candy."

"And I'll bet you're just as sweet—easy, girl. I been without long, like we said. I don't want it to end so soon."

"Maybe we better dry you off, mister, and take care of you before you explode."

"Good idea."

John got out of the tub and the girl began to dry him with a towel while the man grinned across at Tracker. When he was dry everywhere but his crotch the girl knelt before him and tenderly dried his balls and cock.

Putting aside the towel she said, "Now." She took John's raging erection in both hands and began to lick the swollen head.

"Shitfire!" he said, closing his eyes.

From behind Tracker watched the play of muscle in the girl's back as her head bobbed up and down. She was taking more and more of John's dick in her mouth until finally, with a great groan, he came in her mouth and she swallowed his entire emission with no problem.

This gal, Tracker thought—his own cock throbbing inside his pants—is a pro.

"Damn!" John said, shaking his head as the girl sat back on her heels.

"Okay?" she asked.

"That was fine, Candy, just fine. You sure know your business."

She stood up, looked at both men and asked, "Who's paying?"

"My friend," John said, and then got back into the tub to finish his bath.

She turned and walked toward Tracker very deliberately, knowing that he was examining every inch of her.

"What about you, mister?" she asked, eyeing the massive bulge in his pants.

"Yeah, how about you, Tracker?" John asked, grinning.

Tracker studied the girl further, and he could smell her sharp bitch-in-heat scent.

"Turn around," Tracker said to John.

"Hey, you watched me—"

"Turn around."

"There's a closet over there," she told Tracker, indicating the far wall with her eyes. Obviously, she'd plied her trade in this room before.

"Closet?" John said. "Hell, I'm turning around."

"Get in the closet."

"Tracker—"

"Get dried off and get in the closet, or I'll coldcock you and put you in there."

John gave Tracker a sad look, then shook his head and got out of the tub, drying off and mumbling about false modesty. He put his shorts on, picked up the rest of his clothes and walked to the closet.

"It's dark."

"Get in," Tracker said.

John walked into the closet and, without being told to, Candy walked over and shot the bolt, locking him in. She turned to Tracker then, preening, sticking her chest out and clasping her hands behind her back.

Tracker sighed, stood up and undressed. He heard her sharp intake of breath when his rigid cock came into view.

"Mister, you got the biggest—"

"Never mind," he said. "I don't need any of your whore patter. Just come over here and do your job."

64

"Yes sir."

She knelt in front of him, eyes wide, and grasped his huge erection with both hands. She began to lave the bulbous head, lubricating it well before allowing it to slide past her lips into her mouth. He grasped the back of her head as she accommodated more and more of him, and then she began to bob her head and do her job, cupping his balls in her hand.

When Tracker felt that he could take no more of her expert attention he said, "That's enough."

She allowed him to slide free and then looked at him through unfocused eyes. "But, you're not—" she began breathlessly.

"Get on your back," he said, and she eagerly complied.

He mounted her, slammed himself home and began to pound into her with no thought of anything but his own release. She wrapped her fleshy legs around his hips and began to match the tempo of his thrusts. She grunted, moaned, snorted and made every noise a human could possibly make as he banged away, and when he finally exploded inside her she did something not many whores do on the job—she had an orgasm. And not *just* an orgasm, because as her body was racked with shockwaves of pleasure, she screamed, making Tracker's ears ring...

"Oh, mister..." she said as he stood up, leaving her spread-eagled on the floor.

Tracker picked up his pants, took out some money and said, "Here."

She sat up, struggled to her feet and accepted the money. He noticed that her large breasts had absolutely no sag and wished he had the time to pay them more attention.

"Get dressed and get out."

"You're pretty hard, huh, mister?" she asked, picking up her dress and putting it on.

"You should know."

She walked to the door, then turned and said, "Candy. Remember my name, mister, in case you, uh—"

"I'll remember."

She gave him one last look, and then left the room.

"Tracker!" John called from the closet.

"What?" Tracker called. He set about to changing the water in the tub.

"What did you do, kill her?"

Tracker didn't answer.

"Hey, you out there?"

"Yeah."

"Well, let me out."

Tracker got into the tub and called out, "I'm in the tub."

"Tracker!"

"Relax a while, friend," Tracker said. Sitting down in the tub of hot water he added to himself, "That's what I intend to do."

The rest of the bathing went off without a hitch and by the time they had dressed and gotten back to their rooms, Heck Thomas had arrived. Tracker was trying to figure out how to immobilize John when there was a knock on the door. He assumed correctly that it was Heck.

"That was quick," Tracker said as the detective stepped past him into the room.

"They were pretty close on our tails."

"Were?"

"That's the funny part, Tracker," Heck said, frowning. "While I was watching them they stopped and then suddenly turned around and went back."

"Went back?"

"I don't understand it either," Heck said, "but I've got a theory."

"Let's hear it."

"It all depends on your answer to a question."

"What question."

"How easy was it for you to break Barlow and John, here, out?"

"Too easy," Tracker said, nodding.

"We're thinking the same thing, then."

"We sure are."

"The warden let us escape," John said, and both of the other men looked at him.

"So we're *all* thinking the same thing," Tracker added.

"Three great minds," John said, drawing a scowl from Heck Thomas.

"If that's the case," Heck went on, "then we've got nothing to worry about from a posse."

"Was there a lawman with them?"

"Not that I could see."

"Then the warden simply sent some of his people after us to make it look good. The sheriff in Huntsville might still get a posse together, but they'd be too far behind us to worry about."

"I agree," Heck said.

"Me, too," John added.

"Shut up!" Heck told him. John subsided, but Tracker noticed he still had that bemused grin on his face, as if he knew something they didn't.

"Let's not get too confident here," Tracker said, warning himself and Heck.

"What do you suggest?"

"I think we should travel cautiously, as if we did have a posse on our trail."

"Play it safe, you mean?"

"Right. If nothing else it will keep us alert for any other kinds of trouble, as well."

"I don't usually like playing it safe," Heck Thomas said, "but I guess it makes sense."

"Don't you fellas have enough to worry about with creating a phantom posse?" John spoke up, alternating glances between the two. "You've still got the Barlows ahead of you, you know."

"We'll worry about the Barlows when the time comes—" Tracker started to say, but John seemed to know what was coming and cut him off before he could go any further.

"I know, I know," John said, holding his hands up in front of him, "you want me to just shut up and take care of my part."

"You've got that right," Heck said. "Look," he went on, directing himself to Tracker, "you fellas have had a bath; now I'm going to go and get one. After that, I want to try and get a fresh horse."

"All right, you get your bath and your horse and we'll meet you at the nearest eating place."

"What if it's a pigsty?" John asked.

Tracker looked at John and said, "It'll still be better than what you were eating in Huntsville."

John grinned and said, "You've got a point there."

[18]

Tracker and John didn't wait for Heck to arrive at the cafe for dinner and started to eat without him.

"Well," John said as they were eating, "you were right about one thing."

"What?"

"The food's better than it was at Huntsville."

"Yeah, but you were right about one thing, too," Tracker said in return.

"What?"

"It's a pigsty," Tracker said, flicking a dry crust of food off the table that could have been there for an hour or a year.

"My sense of taste can't be trusted yet," John said. "How is the food?"

"Lousy," Tracker said, dropping his fork, "but it won't hurt us because this coffee would kill anything."

"You're not gonna finish yours?"

"No."

"Give it here, then," John said, reaching for Tracker's plate. Tracker's steak was like rubber, and his potatoes were swimming in some kind of grease, but to John it was a big improvement over prison food.

"Your stomach is never going to forgive you," Tracker said, making a face as John stuffed food—or what passed as food in that place—into his mouth.

"I'm touched by your concern."

"Look, John—is there something else we can call you? I'm getting tired of calling you 'John.'"

"What's wrong with John? It's a perfectly good name. It's in the Bible, you know."

"It sounds too much like a name someone would use when he doesn't want anyone to know his real name."

"Didn't you hear Jesse call me John? That's the name I was sent to prison under."

"Yeah, but John what?"

The man concentrated on what he had in his mouth for a moment, then swallowed and said, "I'll tell you what. You can call me J.W."

"What's the W stand for?"

John just smiled and said, "Take your pick."

"All right," Tracker said, "J.W. it is."

At that point Heck Thomas walked in, looked around the room, spotted Tracker and J.W. and walked over to join them.

"This place *looks* like a pigsty," he observed, sitting down. "How's the food?"

"Fine," J.W. said.

"Terrible," Tracker answered.

Heck looked at both of them and then said to Tracker, "Since he's been in prison, I'll take *your* word for it. I'll have some coffee, though."

Heck poured himself a cup, sipped it and immediately made a face.

"Jesus."

"Drink it," Tracker said. "If you're coming down with anything, that'll kill the germs."

Heck gave Tracker a doubtful look, but took another sip of coffee. It didn't seem as bad the second time around.

"We were just discussing names," Tracker said, and went on to explain that John had confided that he could be called J.W.

"Is that a fact? Well, I don't really care what he wants to be called—ah, the hell with it. You call him whatever you like."

"Heck," J.W. said, "somehow I get the feeling we're just never going to see eye to eye."

"I have a way we can see eye to eye right now," Heck explained.

"How's that?"

"Tell us where we're going."

The man who was known as either John or J.W. looked at both men as they studied him expectantly, then leaned back and folded his arms across his chest.

"I'll tell you this much," he said finally, "we are going into Mexico."

70

"I'd have never guessed," Tracker said.

"If I tell you more than that you won't need me anymore," the man explained, "and I just am not ready to go back inside yet."

Heck looked at Tracker in disgust and the big man just shrugged.

"I'm gonna find someplace else to eat," Heck said. "I ain't happy with the food here," he added, looking at J.W., "or the company."

"What's he got against me, anyway?"

"I'm not sure. I guess it just goes against the grain of a man like him to break a convict out of prison. He's used to putting men like you in there, not helping you get out."

"Maybe he just feels guilty about Jesse getting killed and he's taking it out on me."

"I doubt that."

"Why? Don't you feel even a little twinge of guilt about the kid getting killed?"

"No."

"If you had left him inside he wouldn't be dead right now."

"Can you guarantee me that?"

For the first time since they'd met J.W. looked unsure of himself.

"No, I can't."

"He got himself put into prison, not me," Tracker went on. "He got himself into a situation where he ended up getting killed, not me. Look at you, J.W. You got yourself thrown into jail, didn't you? You didn't need any help."

"Jesus, Tracker, you don't even know if I'm guilty or not."

Tracker laughed and said, "J.W., I never met a man who was in prison who *was*."

[19]

There were only three customers in the cantina in the Mexican town of Red Sand, and they were three of the Barlow brothers. Jud Barlow was up on the roof, keeping a lookout for either a posse or their youngest brother, Jesse.

Aside from the Barlows the only other people in the cantina were the bartender, the guitar player, and two Mexican saloon girls dressed in peasant blouses and skirts.

"Three more beers, bartender," Red Barlow called out. He was the oldest of the five brothers, and the smartest and so by default he was the leader.

"Please, señor," the portly bartender cried out, "let some of my other customers come in. I cannot stay in business this way."

"You'll stay in business as long as we let you," Steve Barlow told the man. Aside from Red, he was the oldest and Red's right-hand man.

"But señors, you do not pay—"

"Shut up!" Jim Barlow shouted, throwing an empty whiskey bottle toward the bar. The bartender ducked, silently praying that the bottle would not hit the mirror. When it bounced harmlessly off the wall without even shattering he breathed a sigh of relief and proceeded to draw three more beers for the crazy *Norte Ameri-canos*.

"Red, how long are we gonna keep waitin' here?" Jim demanded unhappily.

"Until Jesse shows up."

"The kid's in Huntsville, for Christ's sake," Jim said. "We got all that money just sittin'—"

"Shut up!" Steve Barlow shouted at his brother. "We don't need nobody knowin' where that money is."

Steve had one of the Mexican girls on his lap, and the other was seated next to him. From time to time he'd take one or the other—and one time both—upstairs to one of the rooms and then come back down and sit with them while he drank. When they turned in for the night he took one of them with him to his room, unless he was on watch. That was one of the things that made Jim so mad at his brother—but it was only one of the things.

"Don't shout at me!" Jim Barlow shouted, knocking his chair over as he jumped to his feet. "I'll pull that Mexican whore off your lap and—"

"Shut up!" Red Barlow shouted.

On the other hand, Jim Barlow was afraid of his brother Red, because Jud Barlow did anything Red said, and Jim was deathly afraid of Jud because Jud was huge. Jim knew that, even though he was six feet tall, Jud could pick him up and break him in half like a twig—and would if Red said to!

"Red, he can't always talk to me like that—"

"Go upstairs and relieve Jud, Jim," Red said, "and then you won't have to listen."

"It's not my turn—"

"Go anyway!"

"Yeah, sure, Red," Jim said, backing away, "whatever you say."

He went up the steps to the next floor, from where he'd make his way to the roof to relieve Jud, who he secretly thought of as "the idiot."

"You know," Steve said, "he thinks Jud's an idiot, but he's more of a—"

"Shut up!"

Steve Barlow started at his brother's voice, but knew better than to talk back. He, too, knew the strength of their brother, Jud, and feared it.

"I think it's time for us to go upstairs, ladies," Steve said. The girl on his lap—Consuelo—started to get off, but stopped when Red Barlow said, "No."

She looked at Red Barlow's scarred face and once again shivered, but the shiver was not caused by fear, or revulsion, but rather by lust. It was Red Barlow that

73

both girls—Consuelo and her sister, Angelica—wanted to take to their bed, but he did not seem interested. All of the Barlows were dangerous in their own way, but it was Red Barlow who controlled them all, and both women were drawn to his power.

"What—"

"Wait until Jud comes down," Red said. "We've got to talk."

"About what?" Steve asked. "You want to wait for Jesse, we'll wait for Jesse. I got no problem with that, Red."

"You've got no problem with anything, do you, Steve?"

Red loved all of his brothers—in his own way—but Jesse was the only one he could ever really talk to, the only one besides himself who had any brains.

"If he doesn't show up in another week, Steven," Red said, "we're gonna go and get him."

"You mean, break him out of Huntsville prison?"

"That's what I mean."

"What about the others—"

"What do you think I want to talk to—" Red began, but then decided to forget it. "I'll tell you what, Steve. Why don't you just go upstairs with your girlfriends and fuck your brains out. That shouldn't take too long."

"Okay, Red, I'll—" Steven began, but then his brother's exact words sank in and he stared at him with a puzzled frown on his face.

"Go ahead, Steve."

Steve pushed Consuelo off his lap, gave his brother one more puzzled look, then put one arm around each girl and started up the steps. On the way the three encountered Jud coming down and they all had to squeeze to one side to let the hulk of a man by. As he eased by he pressed up against Consuelo's full breasts and leered at her, scaring her half to death as he always did.

"Sit down, Jud," Red said as the big man approached the table. The bartender had put three beers on the table, and Jud downed one of them like it was a shot glass of whiskey.

"Thanks for sending Jim up to relieve me early, Red," Jud said. "I was getting thirsty."

"Sure, Jud, sure."

74

Red studied his simpleminded brother, marveling at how God—if there was such a being—had compensated his brother for his lack of brains by giving him size. Jud Barlow was six-foot-eight if he was an inch, three hundred pounds if he was an ounce—which is about how much brain he had. Still, he never argued the way Steven and Jim did. He was the only one who did *what* he was told *when* he was told. Next to Jesse, Red found that he would rather spend time with Jud than the other two.

"Jud."

"Yeah, Red?" Jud asked, peering at his brother over the second mug of beer.

"What would you say to us going back to Texas and breaking Jesse out of jail?"

Jud Barlow belched loudly, then grinned and said, "When do we leave?"

[20]

Tracker and Heck Thomas decided that the best way to ride was with J.W. between them, whether they flanked him, or rode one in front and one behind.

"You know, you fellas ought to relax where I'm concerned," J.W. told them at one point.

"Oh yeah? Why?" Heck asked.

"Because I'm not going to go anywhere," J.W. explained. "It serves my purpose to ride along with you fellas."

"And what purpose is that?"

"I don't want to be a hunted man all my life. If I can help you recover that money maybe I can get a reduced sentence or even a pardon."

Heck was staring at J.W. dubiously, but Tracker had a feeling that the man was telling the truth.

"What happens when the shooting starts?" Heck asked. "I'll tell you what happens," he went on without giving J.W. a chance to reply. "First chance you get you'll light a shuck while we're ducking bullets."

"Wrong."

"Oh yeah? Well, enlighten me then. What happens when we start trading lead with the Barlows?"

"That's easy," J.W. said. "You'll give me a gun."

"Jesus—" Heck said, shaking his head in disbelief and disgust.

"I told Tracker back in town, Heck," J.W. continued, "that the time would come when you'll *ask* me to pick up a gun."

"You probably don't even know how to use one."

J.W. just looked over at Tracker and shrugged after that remark, and then looked straight ahead toward Mexico.

"How long are we gonna put up with this horseshit?" Heck demanded of Tracker.

"I don't know about you, Heck," Tracker replied, "but I think that J.W. here really does know where the Barlows are—or at least where Jesse thought his brothers were."

"You're crazy. He's got you buffaloed."

"That may be, but I'm a gambler and I'm playing the cards I've been dealt. You're free to go back if you like."

That suggestion made Heck sit up straight in the saddle and stare at Tracker.

"You'd like that, wouldn't you?" he demanded, then. "You'd recover the money and walk away with the reward *and* the credit."

"Is that what you're after?" Tracker asked. "The credit?"

"I'm after the same thing you are, Tracker," Heck replied. "The money."

"Let's look at it another way, Heck."

"What way's that?"

"If you turn back, I'd have to face the Barlow brothers alone."

"No you wouldn't, Tracker," J.W. spoke up. "You'd have me."

Heck stared first at Tracker and then at J.W., and then slowly shook his head.

"Jesus," he said, "that alone is a good enough reason for me to keep going along with you. You get killed while I'm not around and I'd never forgive myself."

As they continued to ride Tracker and J.W. exchanged glances without Heck noticing. The look on Tracker's face said, "Thanks," and the look on the convict's face said, "It was easy."

They stopped at the first town they came to after crossing the border because there was only another hour or so of light, and the town after was farther away than that.

"We'll get two rooms and I'll keep J.W. with me," Tracker said as they put their horses up at the livery.

"That's fine with me," Heck said. "I'm gonna take a turn around town and see what I can find out."

77

"Like what?" J.W. asked.

"Like whether or not the Barlows passed through here or not."

"You still don't believe me. They passed through this way if they were going where Jesse thought they were."

"I'll believe that—and you—when I see them myself," Heck said.

"Are you this distrustful of all people," J.W. asked, "or just convicts?"

"All outlaws, in prison or out," Heck said. "I'll see you later," he said to Tracker and left.

"You know something?" J.W. said to Tracker.

"What?"

"I really like that fella."

"Why?"

J.W. shrugged and said honestly, "I don't know."

Tracker checked himself and J.W. into the hotel and then decided they'd go and get something to eat. He left Heck to check himself in, as it seemed fairly obvious that the detective wanted to hold onto his independence. To that end they also did not wait for him to eat.

Over dinner J.W. said, "It looks like you keep gettin' stuck with me."

"By choice."

"Oh really? What is it about me that you can't tear yourself away?"

"If I leave you with Heck I don't think you'd last a half an hour without getting killed."

"You might have a point."

"I do," Tracker said, seriously; and the other seemed to realize that he *was* serious.

"I'm touched by your concern."

"Don't be," Tracker replied. "I don't want him killing you before you lead me to that money. After that, he can do what he likes with you."

J.W. studied Tracker for a few moments and then said, "Remember when I said I liked Heck?"

"Yeah."

"The same doesn't apply to you."

"I'm heartbroken."

[21]

Heck Thomas was annoyed.

He was annoyed with himself for several reasons. First of all, he was not in control of this situation, and he was used to being in control. Secondly, he was mad at himself because he was letting J.W., or John, or whatever his damn name was, get to him. He didn't like the man, and he knew that J.W. was playing on that. He was going to have to watch himself in the future.

It was his general annoyance, however, that made him careless, which was something else Heck Thomas was not usually guilty of.

He went into the first cantina he saw, which was crowded with locals, and ordered a whiskey.

"Bartender," he said when the man brought his drink.

"Si, señor?"

"There were no signposts outside of this town," he said. "What's the name of this place?"

"It does not have a name, señor," the man replied sadly. Heck didn't know if the man was genuinely sad, or if he just had that kind of face.

"No name?"

"No, señor."

"Why is that?"

The man shrugged and said, "No one ever bothers to stay in this town long enough to name it."

"You've got no permanent residents?"

"A few, señor," the man said. "Myself, some others, but we do not care if the town does not have a name."

"Why not?"

"Perhaps not so many people will visit a town without a name."

"Don't like visitors, huh?"

The man shrugged. It was obvious that he did not like visitors, but did not want to take a chance of offending Heck.

"Maybe you'd be able to tell me, then, if four men have passed through this way in the past few weeks or so?"

"Gringos?"

"Yep."

The man simply shrugged his reply.

"I do not know, señor."

Heck frowned and asked, "What do you mean you don't know? Why'd you ask if they were gringos?"

Again the man shrugged.

"I get the feeling you just don't like to talk to strangers."

"I mind my own business, señor," the bartender said. "It is a good habit to get into."

"I don't need you to tell me what kind of habits to get into."

"I did not mean to say that, señor."

"Then what did you mean?" Heck pressed.

The bartender looked past Heck at that point and Heck used the bar mirror to look behind him. There was a table with four locals seated at it and they seemed to be taking particular interest in the conversation at the bar.

"Are those fellas permanent residents, too?"

"Señor?" the bartender said, jerking his eyes back to Heck's face.

"Those four yahoos at that table seem mighty interested in what we're saying."

"You would not want to talk to them, señor. You would do better just to leave. I will not charge you for the drink—"

The bartender stopped short all of a sudden and, again using the mirror, Heck saw that the four men had stood up and were approaching the bar. He cursed himself for walking into the place alone and not checking it out carefully before staying and asking questions. He should have noticed those four when he first walked in, but he'd been preoccupied.

Ever since he met Tracker, he'd just been doing everything wrong!

"Your pardon, señor," one of the men said. Heck used the mirror to study the man. He was large—bigger than Heck himself—but he was soft in the belly and had heavy, unshaven jowls. He also had several gold teeth in the front of his mouth, and his breath smelled of cheap tequila.

"Are you talking to me?" Heck asked, without turning his head to look at the man. He was flanked by the four men, two on one side and two on the other. Not an enviable position if they had anything else in mind besides talk.

"Si, señor, I was," the man said. "You seem to be asking Carlos many questions. I would like to know what they are about."

"Is that a fact?"

"Si, señor," the man said again.

"Why?"

"Señor?"

"Why is it any of your business what we were talking about?"

"Perhaps you do not understand—"

"No, I don't," Heck said, cutting the man off. "Why don't you explain it to me." To the bartender he said, "Give me a bottle."

As the bartender placed a bottle of whiskey on the bar the spokesman for the four said, "Our town does not have a name, señor, and it does not have a mayor, or a sheriff. In the absence of these things I am—what would you call it—in charge by default?"

"In charge?"

"Si," the man said, smiling broadly. "I am, ah, unofficially the mayor, and the sheriff."

"I see."

"I am glad you see, señor. Now, what is it you were talking to Carlos about?"

Heck paused, very deliberately pouring himself a drink from the bottle, and then without looking at the man said, "None of your business." He did not bother to remove his left hand from around the bottle.

The man's face clouded and his gold teeth disappeared from sight as his mouth stretched tightly.

"Carlos!" he snapped.

The bartender jumped at the sound of his name.

81

"He was asking about four gringos passing through town, Chico."

"Ah," Chico said, as if he suddenly understood, "the four American bank robbers."

Heck's eyes flicked over to the man, again using the mirror, and pinned him with a hard stare.

"Who said anything about bank robbers?"

"Oh, one of the four men you speak of boasted very loudly about it."

"Then they did pass through here."

"Si, señor, they did, and my friends and I would like very much to find them again." The man called Chico laid one meaty hand on Heck's left shoulder and said, "You will take us to them."

"What makes you say that?"

"Because, my friend," Chico said, "there is plenty of money to go around...and," he added, tightening his grip on Heck's shoulder, "if you do not agree, you will not leave this cantina alive."

The man was waiting patiently—and confidently—for Heck's reply, and Heck decided that the time for being careless was over.

In one smooth motion he whipped the whiskey bottle off the bar and smashed it over Chico's head. Without waiting to see the effect the blow had he drew his gun and whipped it in an arc, slicing open the cheek of one of the men on his right side.

That done he pushed himself away from the bar, backpedaling away from the remaining two men who had been prepared to grab for him. Realizing that he was gone from their reach both men started to go for their guns, but Heck's was already in his hand.

"Don't try it!" he shouted and both men froze, their eyes on the detective's gun.

Chico, their leader, was down on one knee, staggered and bleeding from several facial cuts. The other man Heck had struck down was on all fours, blood leaking from his face soaking into the hard-packed dirt floor of the cantina.

"I suggest you fellas pick up your self-appointed mayor, sheriff and king and your other friend and get them out of here. They need a doctor's care."

The two men slowly straightened from a crouch and

one moved toward Chico while the other assisted the second man to his feet.

The bartender, Carlos, was in shock, mouth agape, as he watched the four men leave the saloon. When they were gone Heck Thomas holstered his gun, approached the bar and downed the drink he had poured for himself.

"Well," he said to the bartender, who backed away a few steps as Heck looked at him, "I guess I got the answer to my question. Gracias."

The town didn't have a name, it didn't have a mayor, or a sheriff, but one thing it did have was a doctor, and he was working on the facial cuts of unofficial, self-appointed mayor/sheriff Chico Mendez.

"Are you finished?" Chico demanded angrily.

"Almost," the elderly doctor said, applying a bandage to the deepest cut, just above the left eye. "I only wish I had been there to see the man who did this to you."

"You don't worry about that man," Chico said, looking at his three cohorts, one of whom was sporting a bandage on his cheek. "That man is going to lead us to a lot of money and then we are going to take it from him—and we will take his life, as well! This I swear!"

"You look particularly pleased with yourself," Tracker said to Heck.

"I'm not," Heck said. He had found Tracker and J.W. at the cafe where they were eating after checking into the hotel.

"Something went on."

"It did," Heck said, and went on to explain to both men what had occurred.

"Sounds like you had an exciting time," J.W. observed.

"It also sounds like we'll have to leave town sooner than we had planned," Tracker said.

"Why?" J.W. asked.

"My friend Chico won't let me get away with what I did to him," Heck explained. "I think one of us will have to stay awake and alert at all times tonight," he said, directing this remark to Tracker.

"I volunteer for the first watch," J.W. said quickly.

"I suppose you'd like us to give you a gun, too?" Tracker asked.

"Just in case of trouble," J.W. said.

"I think Heck and I will be able to handle the watches, J.W.," Tracker said. "Thanks all the same."

[22]

The night passed uneventfully. Once or twice Tracker thought he noticed someone across the street, watching the hotel from a darkened doorway. It was not until morning that he mentioned it to Heck and the detective mentioned that he, too, thought he might have seen someone.

"Well, if we both did, then there must have been someone there," Tracker said.

"So that's their game, then," Heck said.

"What?"

"They're going to watch us, probably try to follow us and, when we find the money, take it away from us."

"Those four? I don't think they could."

"If they want it bad enough, they can figure out a way," Heck said.

"Yeah, I suppose you're right. We'd better be especially alert from here on in."

"I wish we knew how much further we had to go," Heck said, looking across the room at J.W.

"Don't look at me like that," the man said, matching Heck Thomas's stare. "I'm just looking out for myself. You wouldn't do it any differently, Heck."

"No," Heck said after a moment, "I don't suppose I would."

Heck left the room—and the hotel—to get the horses ready, and J.W. got to his feet and walked up next to Tracker.

"We may be in worse trouble than we thought," he said.

"Why do you say that?"

"That's the first time Heck ever agreed with me," J.W. said, looking genuinely puzzled.

Heck brought the horses to the front of the hotel, and once again the supplies he had purchased were distributed equally among the saddlebags. He and J.W. had fresh horses, while Tracker still rode Two-Pair.

"We're sure wearing horses out in bunches, J.W. and me," Heck said.

"Only he knows how many more you'll wear out," Tracker observed.

"That horse of yours sure has a lot of stamina," Heck commented with admiration as they were riding out of town. "Where'd you get him?"

"I won him in a poker game," Tracker said, patting Two-Pair's neck affectionately.

Heck shook his head and said, "Everything in life should come that easy."

Tracker looked at him and said, "Who the hell said it was easy? I named him after the winning hand, and I had to bluff out a flush to do it!"

When Red Barlow left the cantina his brother Jim was drinking and brooding, big Jud was on the roof and Steve was on the second floor putting it to his two Mex whores—which was what brother Jim was brooding about. There were two other members of the Barlow family in town, though, and Red Barlow was on his way to check up on them now.

The five Barlow brothers had two younger sisters who were not gang members, but they were family members, and since the death of their parents Red— as head of the family and the gang—insisted that they be taken wherever the brothers went. Red also insisted, however, that they be kept out of their robberies. In addition to the fact that the girls would just get in the way, he was trying to keep his sisters' pretty faces off of wanted posters.

They had put the two girls up in a small boarding house on the edge of town, and Red checked in with them from time to time to see if they needed anything.

They always did, but he never gave it to them.

The only problem Red had with his sisters was that they weren't afraid of him, or any of their other brothers, not even huge Jud. (Red had heard the two girls on one occasion describe Jud as "cute.") For that reason, they were harder to keep in line.

Sometimes Red Barlow thought he made a good bank robber, but he wasn't cut out to be a substitute father.

[23]

They rode for most of the morning and when they stopped to give the horses a blow Tracker said to Heck Thomas, "What do you think?"

"I think we should just assume that they're there and stop worrying about it. They're not gonna do anything until they think we have the money."

"I think you're right," J.W. said.

Both men looked at him and then Heck Thomas said something that had been on his mind ever since meeting this man—which he himself had only just realized.

"You know what really bothers me about you?"

"My good looks?"

Heck ignored the remark. J.W. was only a few years younger than Heck Thomas, but he looked ten years younger—because Thomas looked years older than he actually was.

"I get the feeling that I should know you," he said, peering intently at the man.

At that moment Tracker realized that on more than one occasion he had been staring at J.W. and thinking the very same thing.

Suddenly J.W. seemed to become self-conscious.

"I don't know why you'd say that, Heck," he said, trying too hard for a light mood, "we've never met before—wait, do you have a sister?"

"Don't worry about whether I have a sister or not, friend," Heck said, staring at the man. "It'll come to me soon enough where I know you from."

"Well, when it does," J.W. said, staring off into the distance, "let me know."

"Believe me, you'll be the first."

"I think we'd better keep moving," J.W. said, changing the subject. "We don't have much further to go, if I remember correctly."

"If you remember—" Heck exploded.

"Let's move," Tracker said, before they went into one of their exchanges, "you two can fight when we get there."

"Get where?" Heck asked.

"Wherever this man is taking us," Tracker said, "and he's got about one more day to do it in and then I'm taking him back to Huntsville."

"Well," Heck said, smirking at J.W., "finally, something to look forward to."

"Yeah, well don't look too hard," J.W. said, "because we'll be there before nightfall."

"Finally," Tracker said, "something to look forward to."

As their journey continued Tracker—riding behind J.W. while Heck rode ahead of the man who was technically their prisoner—kept picturing the man's face in his mind, trying to fit a name to it. What Heck had said brought home to him how, unconsciously, he had been trying to place J.W.

It was obvious that the man was somebody beyond John or J.W. These names were all he would offer, and there had to be a reason for that. However, Tracker was aware that his efforts toward that end would have to continue to take place unconsciously because there were more serious matters at hand to be taken care of.

Like finding the Barlow brothers, recovering the money, keeping it from the Mexican gang that was following them—and staying alive!

The cut over Chico Mendez's eye was burning. The doctor told him that meant it was healing, but he thought that meant it hurt, and that reminded him of what he owed the gringo from the cantina.

The man on the horse next to him was Jose Rijo, and the wound on his cheek hurt, too. He couldn't wait for Chico to decide that it was time to kill the gringos— all three of them!

The other two men, Santos Barojas and Alberto Valdez, were there simply because Chico told them they had to be. Everything they did they did because Chico told them to. They had never had one independent thought between them, and probably never would. At the moment they were following the gringo and his friends, waiting for Chico to say it was time to kill them.

"How much longer, Chico?" Jose Rijo asked, touching the bandage on his cheek.

"Be patient, Jose," Chico said, touching the wound over his eye, "my cuts hurt just as much as yours do, but we must wait until they have the money."

"How do we know they even know where the money is?"

"They do not know *now*," Chico Mendez said, "but give them time. These are very determined gringos."

"And how long shall we give them?"

"Long enough."

"And then?"

"You are a bloodthirsty man, Jose."

"Only when my own blood has been spilled," the man replied.

"My blood stained the floor of the cantina also, Jose," Chico reminded him. "Do not worry, my friend. When the time comes we will slit the gringo's throat and watch his blood pour out."

"And his friends?"

"They have done us no harm," Chico said, magnanimously. "We will kill them quickly."

[24]

"There it is."

Tracker and Heck looked down at the town in the valley before them and then looked at each other.

"What's the matter?" J.W. asked.

"You sure that's it, J.W.?" Tracker asked.

J.W. looked around and said, "The lay of the land is the way Jesse described it to me, and so's the town. Yep, that's it, all right."

The town was not large, but it was sprawling. It took up twice as much space as it might have if the buildings were closer together.

"Recognize it?" Tracker asked Heck.

"Yeah, I recognize it, all right."

"What are you fellas talking about? You know this town?" J.W. asked.

"Yeah," Heck said absently, staring down at it. "Tracker, that there's Red Sand."

"It sure is."

"That's it, then," J.W. said, "that's why Jesse said his brother Red picked it, because it had the same name as him."

"You never heard of Red Sand?" Heck asked J.W.

"I've spent a lot of time in Texas, but not much in Mexico," J.W. said.

Heck looked at Tracker, who said, "I've been in Mexico before."

"So who's gonna tell me?" J.W. asked, looking from one to the other.

"It's a town with no law," Heck said. "It never had any and it probably never will."

"So what? The last town we were in had no law."

"And no name," Heck reminded him. "This one's got a name, and a rep."

"What kind of rep?"

"Outlaw town," Tracker said. "A place to hole up and wait out a hot posse."

"Wait a minute," J.W. said, as if suddenly remembering something. "I've heard stories of such a town, but I never heard the name...Red Sand, huh?"

"Yep," Heck said. "We're liable to find more in that town than we bargained for, Tracker."

"Don't I know it."

Heck looked over at J.W., who said, "I'm a problem now, huh? You can't take me back, and if you take me down there I'll be among my own kind, right?"

"He reads minds," Heck said to Tracker.

"Well, you're wrong," J.W. said.

"Tell me how," Heck said.

"We've got to go into that town separately," J.W. said. "We all know that, right?"

"Two and one, at least," Tracker said.

"Sure," J. W. said, "Tracker and me, and then you, Heck—but I've got to go in with a gun, or it's going to look mighty funny."

"Like you said," Heck repeated, "you're a problem."

"I'm trying to tell you that I'm not," the man said. "I'll help you get the money back."

"In return for what?" Heck asked.

"Just speak up for me when we get back to Texas," J.W. said. "Who knows, maybe I'll get a pardon, or at least a reduction of my sentence."

"That's all you want?" Heck asked.

"That's it."

"That and a gun," Tracker said.

"The gun's for your protection," J.W. said. "It'll look funny us riding in and me without a gun."

Tracker and Heck thought it over, and Tracker spoke his mind first.

"You got a spare, Heck? Besides that derringer?"

"I've got an old Navy Colt and a worn holster."

"That'll do," J.W. said.

"Give it to him," Tracker said.

"What?"

"Make sure it doesn't have any bullets in it, though."

"Oh," Heck said, "I get it."

"No bullets?" J. W. said. "What good's a gun with no bullets?"

"Nobody'll know it's not loaded, J.W.," Tracker said. "You'll have a gun on your hip and nothing'll look funny. That's what you were concerned about, wasn't it?"

"Yeah, that's what I was worried about."

Heck dismounted and dug his extra gun out of one of his saddlebags.

"Here, strap it on," he said, handing it to J.W.

They watched the man as he took the gunbelt, strapped it on and then checked the weapon.

"You keep this in fine shape," J.W. said, complimenting Heck.

It was clear to both Tracker and Heck that the man had handled a gun before, and probably well.

"You never know when you'll need an extra gun," Heck said, mounting up again.

"Can we get something else straight before we split up?" Tracker said.

"What?" Heck asked.

Tracker looked at J.W. and said, "Can we get your name straight? So far you've been John and J.W. What's your real name?"

It was obvious from the look on the man's face that he still wasn't quite ready to give them his real name.

"If you tell it to us we'll recognize it, won't we?" Tracker said. "You don't want us to know just who we broke out of Huntsville, do you?"

"Not right now," the man answered. "But it's not really important now, is it? Not with what we've got ahead of us. I'll tell you what. If it comes to a point where it looks like we're as good as dead, I'll tell you."

"Now that's a comfort," Heck said.

"If we do what we've got to do and get away with it, then I'll tell you, too."

Tracker looked at Heck, who thought a second, rubbing his jaw.

"I'm still not buying this whole thing," he said to Tracker, looking at the other man. "All we know is that he brought us to Red Sand, but we still don't know that the Barlow boys are down there."

"I'm just saying that we should all go down there

and find out for sure. I mean, I've come this far with you, I'd like to see it through."

Tracker looked at Heck again and this time the detective just shrugged and nodded.

"All right," Tracker said, "but what can we call you in the meantime? I mean, once we're in town, how are we going to introduce you if it comes to that?"

The man removed his hat, scratched his head, then replaced it and said, "I guess you can just call me Wes."

Tracker and Heck discussed who should go down first. One suggestion was that Heck would go down first while Tracker and Wes camped and waited a few hours before following.

"But even that's going to be pressing it," Tracker said. "They probably don't usually see more than one or two people for days."

"Can I offer a suggestion?" Wes asked.

Tracker looked at him and said, "Hell, why not. You're part of the partnership...for now, anyway."

"I think you and I ought to go in first, Tracker, and Heck should camp up here and come in tomorrow morning. That way there won't be two entries in one day. Of course, the ideal situation would be for all three of us to enter on different days—"

"Can't do that, either," Tracker said. "Three consecutive days of strangers coming into town would just be *too* much."

"I hate to say this," Heck said, "but I think Wes is right. Let's do it his way."

Wes looked shocked for a moment, then smiled and looked at Tracker.

"What do you say?"

Tracker rubbed his jaw and said, "I say that if you fellas agree on one more thing, I'm heading back to Texas."

[25]

Tracker and Wes rode down the main street of Red Sand, walking their horses at a leisurely, unhurried pace. They didn't have to contrive to look tired, because they were, and so were their horses.

"We don't seem to be attracting very much attention," Wes observed.

"Don't worry," Tracker said, "we're being noticed by the people who count, I'm sure."

As they continued down the street both men swept the streets with their eyes while attempting to appear not to. They finally located the livery stable and pulled their horses to a halt in front of it.

An elderly Mexican came shuffling out as they dismounted and Tracker, as planned, did all the talking.

"Señor?"

"We'll be here for a few days," Tracker told the old man, handing him the reins. "Make sure you care for them well. They should be ready to ride at any time."

"Si, señor."

"Who's the local law?" Tracker asked.

"Law, señor?" the man asked, frowning. "There is no law here."

"There's no sheriff? No marshal? No *jefe?*"

"No, señor. Do you not know where you are?"

"We're in Mexico."

"Si, señor, but this is Red Sand. There is no law, and all are welcome here."

"Red Sand?" Tracker repeated, as if hearing the name for the first time. "That's real interesting. Where's the nearest hotel?"

"We have several, señor, and some boarding houses. They are all small, however."

95

"Just direct us to the closest one."

"Si, señor," the man said and, pointing, gave them directions.

"Gracias," Tracker said.

"Por nada, señor."

They followed the man's instructions to a small, one-story adobe structure that turned out to be a hotel with only four rooms.

"Can I get my own room?" Wes asked as they entered.

"Let's see how many they have left."

They approached the clerk, who was sleeping on his crossed arms behind a desk made by laying a door across two barrels.

"Excuse me," Tracker said, rapping on the door next to the man's head.

The clerk lifted his head and peered at Tracker from red-rimmed eyes. He was unshaven, gray-faced, and his age was almost impossible to gauge. He was obviously used to spending his nights inside a bottle.

"How many rooms do you have?"

The man frowned and said, "Four."

"No, how many do you have left?"

The man thought again. "Four."

Tracker turned to Wes and said, "We'll have to share a room."

"That's what I thought."

Big Jud watched the two men as they approached town, and then watched carefully as they rode into town. He watched them go to the livery, and then to the hotel, and never once did it occur to him to go downstairs and tell his brothers about it, because his instructions had been to go up and watch for his brother Jesse, or anyone else who came to town.

So that's what he did—he watched.

The room was barely large enough for the two of them, but then that didn't really matter. If there were more expensive rooms to be had in the town, they wanted it to appear that this was all they could afford. The dodge was that they were on the run and looking for a place to hide out—if anyone asked.

"What now?" Wes asked.

"What would we do normally?"

"Normally? I'd go to the nearest cantina and get a drink and a woman, not necessarily in that order."

"Then let's do that," Tracker said, adding, "but with one minor exception."

"What's that?"

"Let's go to the largest cantina in town, because if the Barlows are here that's where they'd be."

"I don't know if that's where we'll find them," Wes said, "but that's where I'd be, so let's go."

[26]

They took one turn around the town on foot and were struck even more by how rambling it actually was. Not a large town as far as its number of buildings, it nevertheless took up the space of a normally settled town three times its size.

"These buildings look like they were dropped here haphazardly," Tracker said. "I've never seen a town set up this way."

"It looks like it was built in stages," Wes said. "I mean that some of these buildings are a lot older than the others. This was probably a tiny little town once, and they've just added a building at a time until they ...built it up to this?"

"I know what you mean," Tracker said. "They finally had to give up."

They passed several small cantinas, but finally came to what had to be the largest one in town.

"This has got to be it," Wes said.

Tracker agreed.

"It's the only two-story building in town."

"Did you see the man on the roof?" Wes asked.

"I saw him, and I think I know who he is."

"So do I. Jesse described him to me enough times."

"Big Jud."

"Can't be anybody else. It's either him or a Ponderosa pine."

"Let's go inside and meet the rest of the family."

"I'm ready," Wes said. "I'd be a lot more ready if I had bullets in my gun."

"You've got them on your gunbelt," Tracker said, "that's close enough."

Since he'd strapped on the gun Wes had not been out

of Tracker's sight, so he'd had no chance to transfer any of those bullets from the gunbelt to the gun.

They walked through the batwing doors together and found themselves in a large, almost empty room. The only occupants of the room were the bartender and one lone man seated at a table, drinking. The man bore enough of a resemblance to the deceased Jesse Barlow for both men to feel excited.

They'd found at least two of the Barlow boys, one on the roof and one inside the cantina.

They walked directly to the bar where the bartender seemed unusually happy to see them—but then again, business was obviously less than brisk.

"Señors," he said. "What can I get for you?"

The bartender's voice seemed to make the man at the table aware of Tracker and Wes's presence, and he looked up at them curiously.

"Beer," Tracker said.

"And a woman," Wes added.

"Yeah."

When the portly bartender brought them each a beer Wes asked, "What about the women?"

Looking upstairs the bartender said, "We have two, señor. I—I will see if they are ... available."

"Fine," Tracker said.

"Are either of them plump?" Wes asked, hopefully.

"I will see, señor," the man said, somewhat nervously. He came out from behind the bar and rather hesitantly mounted the steps. They watched him until he knocked on the first door at the head of the stairs and entered.

"He's a little nervous, isn't he?" Wes asked. "You'd think I asked him for his sister."

"That might not be so bad."

"His sister?"

"She'd be plump."

Wes had opened his mouth to answer when he looked past Tracker. Tracker turned and saw the bartender coming back downstairs with a girl behind him.

A woman.

She wasn't plump, but she was small and big breasted, and wore a low cut peasant blouse, which created an illusion of plumpness. She had dark skin and black hair,

99

and as she followed the bartender she looked past him and smiled.

At Tracker.

"Well," Wes said, "she'll do."

The bartender got back behind the bar and said, "This is Angelina."

"Buenos dias," she said, smiling prettily. "You want a woman?"

"Yes," Wes answered, although the question was put to Tracker.

"There are two of us, but the other is busy. I can take you together," she said, and then looked at Tracker and said, "Or one at a time."

"Oh," Tracker said, "one at a time." He fleetingly wondered if Wes might not take this opportunity to escape, but dismissed the thought. That was when Tracker realized he'd come to trust the convict.

"Yeah," Wes said, putting his beer down and getting ready to go.

"Wait a minute," Tracker said, putting a big hand on his chest. "Where are you going?"

"Upstairs with this lovely lady."

"No, no," Tracker said. "You went first last time."

"When?"

"With Candy, during your bath."

"That doesn't count," Wes complained. "She only—"

"First is first, friend," Tracker said, patting Wes on the chest. He looked at Angelina and said, "Lead the way."

She smiled broadly, grabbed him by the hand and led him up the stairs. He started to put his hand on the doorknob of the door he'd seen the bartender go into but she pulled on his other hand and said, "No, not there." She sounded frightened.

She led him to another door and into an empty room with a bed and a dresser.

"Who's in the other room?"

"Señor Barlow," she said, and made a face. "He is a pig, but we must be nice to him."

"He let you leave to come downstairs?"

"He said I must make a living, but that when I am finished I must come back to him and Estralita."

"Estralita?"

"The other girl."

"Ah."

"You, señor," she said, eyeing him appreciatively, "you are not a pig."

"No."

"You want me?"

"Yes."

Tracker figured that since they had come in asking for beer and a woman—as many men would, coming in off the trail—it would have seemed suspicious for him not to go upstairs with her, and even more suspicious for him not to go to bed with her.

Besides, he wanted this dark-skinned, dark-haired woman, and his cock was twitching with anticipation.

"Yes," she said, looking at his crotch, "you want me."

She crossed her arms in front of her, grasped the bottom of her peasant blouse and peeled it up over her head. She stopped like that, with her hands over her head, and he examined her beautiful, full, smooth-skinned breasts. Her copper-colored nipples were already distended. Her breasts jutted toward him, and then she pulled her blouse off and dropped her arms to cup her breasts in her hands, offering them to him.

Tracker moved toward her, took her breasts in his hands; she leaned into his touch. He lifted those firm orbs to his mouth, licking the flesh around the nipples, and then concentrating on the nipples themselves. At the same time he hooked his thumbs in her skirt and peeled it down to her ankles, then stripped off her underpants. On his knees in front of her he kissed her belly, then ran his tongue down over her dark mound and probed until he could taste her juices.

"Señor, señor," she breathed, thrusting her hips toward him. "Por favor, señor."

"Yes?" he asked, looking at her.

She cupped his face in her hands and said, "I wish you to—how do you say—fuck me?"

"Yes," he agreed, "that's how you say it." He buried his face in the valley between her lush breasts, breathing her musky fragrance.

"Angelina, do they ever call you Angel?"

"No."

"Why not?"

She gave him a sexy smile and said, "Because I am not."

Tracker got to his feet and undressed while she watched. She covered her mouth with her hands when she saw his huge pulsing cock, and then threw herself down on the bed, laughing with delight.

"A real man," she said, pushing one hand down to her pussy. "Not an animal like that cabron, Barlow."

He joined her on the bed, covered her body with his, holding his weight on both hands so he wouldn't crush her.

"Señor, I want your weight. I want all of you—"

He cut her off by slowly pushing past her splayed cunt lips with the head of his cock and entering her slowly, inch by inch.

"Oh, señor," she whispered, wrapping her arms around him, "this is heaven, no?"

"This is heaven," he said, "yes."

"You took your time," Wes said when Tracker joined him at the bar and ordered a beer.

"You don't rush with a woman like that."

Tracker noticed that there was still only one other person in the cantina, the man at the table.

"Yeah, well—" Wes said, stepping away from the bar.

"Where are you going?" Tracker asked, grabbing him by the arm.

"Upstairs. Angelina's waiting for me."

"No, she's not."

"What?"

"She had to go back to Steve Barlow's room."

"Barlow?"

"Seems he's been keeping her and the other girl pretty busy."

"Yeah, but...it's my turn."

"Not tonight."

"Look—"

Wes started to turn, but Tracker stopped him with his shoulder.

"Hey!" the man at the table shouted.

Tracker turned, beer in hand.

"Are you talking to me?"

"Yeah, big man," the stranger replied. "I'm talking to you. What are you doing in this saloon?"

"I'm having a beer," Tracker said. "Are you the owner of this place?"

"Shit," the man said, "I wouldn't own this barn."

"In that case, I don't think I have anything further to explain to you," Tracker said, and turned his back on whichever Barlow the man was.

"Hey, big man," he heard the man say. The scraping of chair legs on the floor told him that the man had stood up. "I'm talking to you!"

"I'm not talking to you," Tracker said without looking back.

"Why you—"

There was the sound of a chair striking the floor and then quick, angry steps as the man approached him. Tracker still wasn't sure how he was going to play it when a voice stopped all the imminent action.

"Jim!" the voice barked out, and there was power enough in it to stop everyone short, and not just the man it was directed at.

Everyone turned to the batwing doors and looked at the man standing there. He was tall, an inch or so over six feet, with broad shoulders and flaming red hair. It was obvious that this was Red Barlow.

"Red, keep out—"

"No," Red Barlow barked, "you get out! This fella here would have broken you into little pieces if I hadn't come in just now."

"Damnit, Red!" Jim Barlow screamed, his face beet-red. The combination of whiskey and his brother's words were bringing him dangerously close to apoplexy.

"Just get out, Jim," Red said, wearily.

The brothers matched glares for several seconds and then Jim Barlow stomped past Red and out of the cantina.

Red Barlow approached the bar as Tracker, with his back to it, leaned his elbows on it and swirled the remainder of his beer in the mug. Wes moved a few feet down the bar to give the two big men room. The bartender closed his eyes and wished he'd had a few more seconds before Red's arrival to collect his money for the two beers.

"Bartender," Red said, and the man behind the bar knew this was a signal for a beer. Red Barlow had never even taken the trouble to learn the man's name. It had simply never occurred to him that the man might have one.

"Sorry about my brother's manners, friend," Red Barlow said when he had his beer.

"That's all right," Tracker said. "A man can't be responsible for his brother's actions."

"I can," Barlow said. "I've got four of them, and I'm responsible for all of them. It gets to be a real chore, sometimes."

"I guess."

"You got any brothers?"

Tracker paused a moment. "No."

"In some ways you're lucky."

"I guess I've got to take your word for that."

"Yeah," Red said. He chugged his beer, put the empty mug on the bar and then said, "You gonna be in town a while?"

"Maybe."

"We'll run into each other again, then."

"I guess."

Red waved and went the same way his brother did.

Wes moved back down the bar near Tracker and they both stared after Red Barlow. Wes started to talk, but Tracker put up a hand to stop him and ordered two more beers. This time the bartender collected his money for both rounds, and couldn't believe his luck.

Tracker and Wes took their beers to a table, where they could talk without being overheard.

"That was strange," Wes said.

"At least we know three of them are here for sure, and probably the fourth."

"It doesn't look like they get along, but then Jesse said that his brothers spent a lot of time going at each other. He said that he and Red were really the only ones who ever got along."

"Red's smart."

"Why do you say that?"

"His brother Jud is on the roof for some reason, right?"

"Yeah, a lookout."

"But neither of the two brothers we just met—Red

104

and Jim—knew we were here. They were surprised, and if that's the way Red Barlow reacts when he's surprised he's a dangerous man."

"Too calm?"

"Right. He's going to talk to the brother on the roof and find out what direction we came from. He'll talk to all of his brothers before he talks to us again."

"And then what?"

"I don't know," Tracker said, making wet circles on the table with the bottom of his mug. "I guess we're just going to have to wait and find out."

Red Barlow found his sulking brother, Jim, in the boarding house where they and Jud had their rooms. Red had put the girls in a separate place, and Steve had taken to sleeping in the cantina with his Mexican whores.

Red walked into brother Jim's room without knocking and said, "Get that idiot down off the roof."

"Who?" Jim asked, looking up from his seated position on the bed.

"Your brother, Jud, you idiot."

"Red—"

"And then get Steve from the cantina and tell him we all have to talk—and go in the back door of the cantina so nobody sees you."

"But Red—"

"Jim, don't give me a hard time right now, all right?" Red said, cutting his brother's complaints off. "I've got enough on my mind."

"But those two men—"

"Those two men," Red said, loudly, "got into this town without us knowing it, and with Jud up on the roof. Get him down here because I want to find out why."

Grudgingly, Jim got up from his bed and said, "Uh, what if he doesn't want to come down?"

"Goddamnit—" Red snapped. "Throw him over the side and make sure he lands on his fucking head so he doesn't get killed, but get him the hell down here!"

[27]

To Jim Barlow's delight Jud was only too happy to come down off the roof.

"I'm getting real hungry," the big man said.

"Tell that to Red."

Jud went down the back stairway while Jim went to get his brother Steve, who wasn't pleased about the interruption.

"Tell that to Red."

They met Jud out back and together they walked to the boarding house where Red Barlow was waiting.

"What's wrong, Red?" Steve asked as they entered Red's room. "Those two Mex gals are waiting—"

"Let 'em wait!" Red snapped.

Steve, recognizing his brother's mood, lapsed into a wary silence. He hoped Red wasn't about to go off half-cocked.

"I want to talk to Jud first," Red said, "so you two just keep quiet for a while."

"Sure, Red," Steve said. Jim nodded and sat in a straight-backed chair; Steve and Jud remained standing.

"What's wrong, Red?" Jud asked.

It was obvious to anyone who saw the four brothers together that they were brothers, yet in Jud's case the Barlow features all seemed to be exaggerated. His mouth, his nose, his chin, they all seemed to be at least two or three times the size of his brothers'. At six-eight, he stood six inches taller than Red, the next tallest. He had massive hands and shoulders and incredible strength, yet was so simpleminded that he was the gentlest of men—unless Red told him to act differently.

In spite of his fury, Red tempered his anger toward

106

Jud. He controlled Jud pretty thoroughly but, knowing Jud had twice his strength, he didn't want to anger him. Instead, when he was angry he scolded Jud, the way a father would, and Jud invariably reacted the way a chastised child would.

"Jud, why did I ask you and your brothers to take turns on the roof?"

"We was watching, Red."

"Right, but watching for what, Jud?"

"For Jesse."

"And?"

Jud shrugged and frowned, indicating he was puzzled by his brother's questions.

"We was watching, Red," he said again.

"Jud," Red said evenly, fighting to control his anger, "did you see two men ride into town earlier today?"

"I sure did, Red," Jud said, grinning now, "and I watched them real good, Red, I really did."

Red closed his eyes and remembered his instructions to Jud as he told him to go to the roof. He realized that he had not specifically told Jud to report to him whenever he saw anyone ride into town. Steve and Jim knew that "keep an eye out for strangers" meant to let him know when they saw someone, but Jud was just not mentally able to figure that out.

"Yeah, Jud," Red said, then, "I'm sure you watched them real good."

Jud took this as praise and smiled happily.

"Thanks, Red."

"All right," Red said, looking at Jim and Steve, "we've got two strangers in town. Jim has already had a run-in with them."

"Get whipped, did he?" Steve asked, grinning.

"I didn't get whipped!" Jim snapped. "If Red hadn't interrupted I would've—"

"Probably gotten whipped," Steve said, quickly.

"Damn it, Steve—"

"All right, quiet!" Red said. "I didn't ask you to come here to argue."

Jim and Steve exchanged glances, but kept quiet and waited for their older brother to tell them why he *had* called them together.

"Jim, think about it. Have you ever seen either one of those men before?"

Jim paused a moment then said, "No, I don't think so. How about you?"

"There's something familiar about that big one," Red said, "but I can't think of it, right now."

"I ain't never seen them before either, Red," Jud chimed in, wanting to be helpful.

"Okay, Jud."

"Maybe they're just a couple of drifters, Red," Steve said, "or maybe they're on the run."

"And maybe they're a couple of lawmen," Red added.

"Did you see a badge?" Steve asked.

"No, but that doesn't mean anything."

"Well, if you're worried that they might be lawmen, why don't we just kill them?"

"Because they may *not* be lawmen, and if that's so, there ain't no reason to kill them."

"Sure there is," Steve said. "Just to be on the safe side."

Red shook his head, indicating he was not pleased with that reason.

"I've just got to think about it a little longer and I'll place that big one."

"How big is he, Red?" Jud asked suddenly. "As big as me?"

"Nobody's as big as you," Red said, and that pleased Jud.

"Steve, we'll have to get you a look at these two and see if you recognize either one of them."

"Want me to go over to the cantina now and take a look?" Steve asked.

"No, not right now. I want them to calm down first after the run-in with Jim. Tomorrow will be soon enough."

"I'm going back to the cantina anyway," Steve said.

"You keep sticking it to those Mex whores," Jim said, "and it's gonna fall off."

Steve grinned at Jim and said, "You're just mad because you ain't even got yours wet in weeks unless you been spittin' on it."

"Why you—" Jim started, standing up, but once again Red stepped in between his two brothers.

"You fellas better calm down or I'm gonna have Jud put you both to bed."

Both Steve and Jim looked from Red to Jud and relaxed.

"Steve, go on back to your whores, but go in the back and don't let those strangers see you."

"You gonna let them keep drinkin' in our saloon?" Jim Barlow demanded.

"For now, yeah," Red said. "When the time comes, we'll let them know that the town is ours, Jim, but I say when the time comes, right?"

"Right, Red."

Red looked at Steve who said, "Hey, right, Red."

Steve and Jim started for the door when suddenly Jud chimed in with, "Right, Red!"

The Barlow sisters—Tess and Bonnie—had been sneaking out of their boarding house when they saw three of their brothers walking from the direction of the cantina to *their* own boarding house.

"What do you suppose that's about?" Tess asked her sister.

"I don't know," Bonnie said, "but maybe they'll be too busy to check on us for a while."

"I hope so," Tess said. "This is like being in a prison without bars."

"Let's go to that small cantina at the other end of town," Bonnie suggested. "Even if they start looking for us it'll take a while for them to get there."

"That's fine with me. I only hope a few strangers have come to town. So far as I've seen, the men in this town are a poor bunch"

Bonnie let out a long sigh and agreed. "It's been so long since I've had a man between my legs I might even settle for one of these local greasers."

"Tessie, I hope we're not that desperate," Bonnie said, eyeing her sister.

"If we ain't," her sister replied, "we're pretty damn close."

"The beer here is terrible," Wes said, pushing his second one away unfinished.

109

"We've got nothing else to do tonight," Tracker said. "Want to try someplace else?"

"Why not? Maybe we'll find a place with a few señoritas? It's been a long time for me..."

Tracker studied Wes and then said, "Well, let's go check it out, then. Maybe we'll both get lucky."

[28]

By the time Tracker and Wes had worked their way down to the smallest cantina in town Tess and Bonnie Barlow had had themselves a couple of drinks. There were a few other men in the place—what the girls referred to as local greasers—but they had not approached the two girls for obvious reasons.

"By now, the boys have all these folks bullied," Bonnie said, "and they wouldn't come near us even if we asked them to."

"Which we ain't," Tess said. "You were right, Bonnie. We ain't that desperate yet."

"Let's have another drink and then head back to our cells."

"Right."

Tess turned to call out to the bartender and at that moment she saw two men enter the room.

"Bonnie!" she whispered.

"What?" Bonnie said. She had not yet seen the two men.

"Look!"

"What?" she asked again, and looked up. "Oh, my!"

"Strangers," Tess said with barely suppressed glee.

Her sister's hand closed over Tess's arm as she said, "Look at the big one!"

"I'm looking, I'm looking," Tess said. "The other one is cute, though."

"To hell with cute," Bonnie said, eyeing the bigger man boldly. "He's like ... like a ... a beautiful, dangerous animal!"

"Take out your little gun, sister dear," Tess said, "it's hunting time."

* * *

111

As Tracker and Wes entered the cantina they immediately spotted the two American women seated at a table.

"Ooh..." Wes said.

"The bar," Tracker said, and they both walked to the bar and ordered a beer.

"What a surprise," Wes said when they had their drinks.

"Good beer, huh?" Tracker said.

"No, I mean the women."

Tracker smiled and said, "I know what you mean."

"What are we waiting for, then? Let's decide who gets who."

There was a mirror behind the bar and Tracker used it to examine the two women.

They were enough alike to be sisters, both with long, dark hair and trim, full-breasted figures clad in jeans and work shirts. The only major difference between the two was that one appeared to be twenty-two or so, while the other couldn't have been more than nineteen.

"Let's be logical about this, Wes," Tracker said. "I'll take the older one."

Wes studied the women in the mirror and then said, "Fair enough. Now which of us is going to go over there and get them to invite us to sit down."

"Don't look now, Wes," Tracker said, watching in the mirror as the older woman approached them, "but I think that's being taken care of."

When the woman came up next to Tracker he was impressed with her height, which had to be close to five-ten.

"You gentlemen are strangers in town, aren't you?" she asked.

"That's right," Tracker said. "We just rode in today. There's not much happening here, is there?"

"There hasn't been," the woman said, looking Tracker right in the eye, "up to now."

"Now?"

"Now that you and your friend are here, I'm hoping that will change," she said. "My name is Bonnie and my sister's name is Tess. We were wondering if you and your friend would like to join us."

112

"At your table?"

"Well," Bonnie said, turning to face Tracker squarely, "that'll do for a start."

After Tracker and Wes had finished their beers they ordered a bottle of whiskey and four glasses. Tracker sat with Bonnie on his left, while Wes sat with Tess on his right. The pairing off had been very easily accomplished right after the introductions were made.

"How long are you fellas planning on being in town?" Tess asked.

"Can't tell right now," Wes said.

"Are you on the run?"

"Let's just say we'd hate to start back the way we came because we might ... run into somebody we don't want to see," Tracker answered.

"Oh," Tess said.

"Besides," Tracker said, looking at Bonnie, "the answer to your question might depend a lot on the rest of this night."

"Is that right?" Bonnie asked, pressing her knee against Tracker's. They each felt that they already had an understanding, and it was just a matter of time ...

"How long have you gals been in town?" Wes asked, directing his question specifically to Tess.

"We've been here a while," Tess said, evasively, "but none of that is important. What's important is tonight. We've been terribly bored up to now, haven't we, Bonnie?"

"That's right," Bonnie said. "It's been a boring town up to now, but we can change that right now, Tracker," she added, closing her hand over his forearm, "can't we?"

"Definitely," Tracker said.

"I think it's time for us to move this party to our rooms," Bonnie said to her sister, "don't you, Tess?"

"If the gentlemen are willing," her sister said, smiling coyly at Wes.

"Willing," Wes told her eagerly, "and very able."

[29]

Each girl had her own room at the small boarding house where they were staying, and according to them their landlady was almost deaf, so they'd have no problem bringing Tracker and Wes into their rooms. Tracker went with Bonnie, while Wes eagerly accompanied the younger sister, Tess.

Tracker and Bonnie regarded each other with interest as they undressed, each impressed by what they saw.

Bonnie saw a tall, well-muscled gent with blond hair and gray eyes, carrying not an ounce of extra weight on his six-four frame. His face was hard and masculine, the way she liked a man's face to be, and his eyes never left her.

He saw a tall, full-bodied young woman with proud, firm, brown-nippled breasts—nipples that were already hardening with anticipation—and a lovely if somewhat angular face, with lush lips filled with promise... and her eyes never left him while she shed her clothes.

"Nobody here is shy," she said frankly.

"No reason to be," he said, dropping the last of his clothes and moving for her.

She met him halfway and their bodies bumped into each other pleasantly.

Tracker slid his big, coarse hands down along the curve of her spine and over the smooth orbs of her behind. Bonnie shivered, both at his touch and because it had been too long since a man touched her like that.

She ran her hands down over his waist, his thighs, and then around front to wrap her fists around the object of her brief search.

"My God," she said, stroking the length of him. "It's incredible."

"So are you," he said, pulling her so tightly against him that the rough black hairs of his chest scraped her sensitive nipples.

"Oh..." she said, and opened her mouth to him. He bent just a bit and took it with his, biting her lush lips and then sliding his tongue in. She moaned; her tongue fenced with his. She maneuvered his long cock between her open thighs and then closed them, trapping it.

They were only a few feet from the bed, but Tracker broke the kiss and lifted her easily, in spite of the fact that she was a big girl.

"My God," she said, running her mouth over his neck as he took two quick steps and then deposited her onto the bed.

"Come on," she said, lifting her arms to him.

"I'm here," he said, getting on the bed with her. She closed her arms around him as he bent his head and began to suck on her nipples, first one and then the other, and then back again, until they were incredibly swollen.

"Mmmm," she moaned, scraping his back with her nails. She tried to reach further down but could not and complained, "I can't reach you."

He lifted his head so he could look into her eyes and then said, "Go ahead, reach me."

She slithered down until her face was level with his crotch, and he rolled onto his back with great anticipation. Bonnie wasn't shy by a long shot. He was sure she knew exactly what she was doing—and he was looking forward to it.

Her tongue came out and rolled around the head of his cock teasingly, wetting it, flicking at the underside. Slowly she began to run her tongue up and down the entire length of him and then she moaned and reached to wrap a fist around the base with one hand, and cup his balls with the other. He saw her eyes widen with her own anticipation, and then her mouth opened and he watched as the length of him began to disappear inside.

Her head began to bob slowly while she held onto him with her hands, both of which were wrapped around

115

the base of his cock now. As he reached down to cup her head she began to move more rapidly, sucking as she did so, and he felt that familiar rush begin in his legs. As if sensing that he was going to give her all she could handle she moaned and got up onto her knees, as if that would allow her to accept whatever he delivered.

And he delivered...

Wes was impatient, but did not want to seem so. He stood still and watched while Tess undressed.

"Aren't you going to take off your clothes?" she asked.

"You're so beautiful," he said, "I want to watch you first."

She smiled and said, "You're sweet."

Tess quickly removed the remainder of her clothes and stood before him naked.

"Well?" she asked.

She was not as tall nor as full-bodied as her sister, but she was simply a slightly smaller version, as firm and as round in every way. Her nipples were dark brown, like her sister's—although Wes had no way of knowing that—and there was a light flush to her skin, as if she were blushing.

"Oh!" he said as he suddenly realized she was waiting for him to undress.

Wes removed his clothing without hesitation. He was very conscious of the fact that he had lost weight while in prison and was much too thin, but he had been careful to maintain as much muscle tone as he could.

"Oh, my," she said, looking down between his legs. His cock had risen swiftly and fully, the swollen head purple and suffused with blood.

She approached him slowly and touched him fleetingly, setting his engorged penis to prodding the air eagerly. Lightly she ran a fingernail along the underside of his shaft and he closed his eyes, afraid that he would shoot right there and then.

"You're so pale," she said.

Her skin had tanned dark brown from constant exposure to the sun, but it seemed to thrive on it. Instead of being burned tough and leathery, it looked smooth and silky.

He reached out and ran his fingertips over her right

breast, circling the nipples as he savored the texture of her flesh, and then taking the brown nub between his thumb and forefinger and tweaking it gently.

"You like to take it easy?" she asked, staring at him curiously.

"You're just very beautiful."

"You're adorable," she said, and with that she dropped to her knees and touched the tip of her nose to the head of his cock. From that position she reached out with her tongue and flicked at the underside of his penis, causing him to start. It had been so long, he hoped he'd be able to hold back.

God! he thought, as suddenly her mouth engulfed him. She worked on him with her tongue, her teeth, her lips, and suddenly he was pulsing furiously, filling her mouth with years' worth of semen....

Tracker's face was buried between Bonnie's legs and her fingers were wrapped in his thick, blond hair as he licked her avidly.

They had wasted no time in reversing their positions after she had sucked Tracker dry, and now he was doing the same for her.

She tasted incredibly sweet and he drove his tongue into her as deeply as he could, to get as much of her honey as possible. Her hips worked furiously, driving up into his face to meet the pressure of his tongue, and she moaned and rolled her head back and forth on the pillow.

"Oh God, it's been so long..." she cried out, and Tracker was glad her landlady was deaf, because he was going to lick her until she screamed.

Tess's legs were wrapped around Wes's hips as he drove his engorged shaft deeper and deeper with each thrust. After she had swallowed his juices he had immediately pushed her down onto the bed and began to run his mouth over her breasts, devouring them.

God, he thought, I forgot how a woman's flesh tastes ...and that thought reminded him that there were many more delights he'd forgotten about.

He abandoned her breasts and worked his way down to the soaking wet area between her legs. Desperately

117

he began to lick the wetness away, and then thrust his tongue inside of her looking for more. Jesus, but she was sweet...

Eventually his tongue had found her swollen clit and he lingered over it, licking it lovingly, twirling it with his tongue until suddenly she groaned aloud, grabbed his head with her hands and crushed his face against the bristly hairs of her brown muff. She ground her hips against him as he sucked on her, and then she was coming, bouncing up and down on the bed and marveling at how incredible it felt...

Tracker's cock was buried to the hilt inside Bonnie; her powerful legs were wrapped around his waist.

"Oh God yes, Tracker, harder, do it harder, please, God, please...do it, do it, do it..."

"I'm doing it," he told her, reaching beneath her to cup the firm cheeks of her generous ass.

"Don't stop..."

"I'm not stopping, Bonnie," he said in her ear, "not until you beg me to."

"I'm...begging...you...not...to..." she gasped.

"Now," he said, "but wait..." and he increased the tempo with which he was slamming into her.

"Oh, Christ!" she bellowed. "Oh, yesss!"

"That's my sister," Tess told Wes. She was seated astride his hips, with his cock nestled inside of her and her hands flat against his chest, grinding her hips.

"Is she always that loud?" he asked.

"Only when she's really getting it just the way she likes it," Tess said, digging her nails into Wes's chest.

"And what about you?"

"Don't worry," she told him, "I'm getting just what I want. You—" she started, but then stopped as the beginnings of another orgasm began to build inside of her. She increased her speed, whipping her hips back and forth and grinding into him harder. "You don't go down," she said, her eyes widening. "I mean, it's as if you haven't...made love for ages...and you just don't ...get...soft..."

He smiled at her as he felt himself getting ready to explode and said, "You don't know the half of it."

Bonnie was on all fours on the bed and Tracker knelt behind her, the swollen, red tip of his cock poking at her tight little anus.

"First," he said, "we have to wet it a bit."

He drove his shaft into her wet pussy from behind and stoked her fire a couple of times, just to lubricate himself. She moaned and pushed against him with her round butt, wetting the entire length of him. Withdrawing he leaned over and flicked his tongue at the little brown eye between her cheeks.

"Oh, jeez..." she cried.

"Now," he said. He spread her cheeks, placed his tip against the tight rosebud, and with one powerful lunge entered her from behind. It was something she had said she wanted, and he was only too glad to comply.

"Oh, Lord..." she yelled, and he swore to himself that he had never run into a woman who called out to God so much during sex.

He felt her muscles close around him and for a fleeting moment was afraid that he wouldn't be able to get out again. Then he forgot about that as she began to butt him in the stomach with her ass. He grabbed her by the hips and matched her tempo, giving her just what she wanted, and more...

"Oh, goddamn, Wes," Tess cried out, "you're splitting me apart!"

"Christ, Tracker," Bonnie shouted, "you're tearing my insides!"

As it welled up inside of him, Wes knew that this was going to be it, this was going to be the last time for tonight, and he only hoped that, after all the time he'd spent in prison, he had been able to satisfy this young creature.

"This is it, Tess!" he shouted.

"At last!" she said, and as he was filling her up for the last time she said, "I thought you were going to kill me!"

* * *

"Tracker," Bonnie said, "Oh, Tracker..."

At least she had stopped calling for God, he thought as he drove himself into her.

He had her buttocks in his massive hands again, and was controlling her. Bonnie was a big girl and she was not used to being in a man's power, but with Tracker there was nothing she could do. He was big, he was gentle but firm, he had given her everything that she could ever have wanted and more, and she recognized that it was his turn to have what *he* wanted.

But he was driving her crazy now!

They had been going at each other for so long now, yet he could still fan a fire inside of her, only it was becoming so exquisitely painful that she knew what he had meant by making her beg him to stop.

This just felt too good to be real!

"Oh, Tracker," she sighed weakly, wrapping her arms around him and using the strength of her arms and her legs to hold him close, "oh, Tracker."

He continued to take her in long, slow strokes as her insides gripped him in a soft but iron grip. She was amazed—as she had been before—that a man his size, with his strength, could be so gentle, yet cause such sensations by *being* gentle.

"Tracker, Tracker," she moaned, feeling the perspiration roll down her face. A drop paused on the tip of her nose and Tracker licked it off. It was such a simple, easy thing to do, yet it seemed to increase the sensations ...no man had ever done to her the things that Tracker had done... was doing...

"Tracker, I can't—"

"Can't what?" he asked.

"Take it—we have to stop, after this time ... we have to stop..."

"Stop?" he asked. "You mean you've had enough?"

"Yes, damn it!" she snapped, almost desperately. "I surrender," she said. "I never thought I'd ever say this to a man—oh, Jesus!—but I've had enough..." she said, and then after the space of one heartbeat she added, "...that is, for now."

[30]

Heck Thomas had taken a while to find just the right spot to camp. An excellent tracker, he now used his skills to ensure that *he* couldn't be tracked to the hole he had picked to spend the night in. The next morning he'd ride down into Red Sand and see what kind of trouble Tracker and Wes had gotten themselves into.

He had worked on the assumption that they were still being tracked by Chico and his friends and although he doubted that the Mexicans would move against him during the night, he wanted to make certain they wouldn't. He hoped once they lost his sign they'd simply assume that all three Norte Americanos had gone into town.

After that, the next move was up to them. Maybe they'd go down into Red Sand and get themselves killed.

Settled in his camp and munching on beef jerky, Heck stared down at the scattered lights of the town and wondered what Tracker and Wes were doing at that very moment.

Chico Mendez fumed silently as he realized that the trail was lost.

"It is getting dark, Chico," Jose Rijo told him. "Perhaps in the morning we will be able to recover—"

"Be silent," Chico said in annoyance. "They have either gone down the valley into that town, or they have hidden themselves from us."

"What will we do?" Jose asked.

"We will camp and wait until morning, and then we will watch," Chico decided. "If they are in that town, they will show themselves soon enough."

"And then what?"

"Eventually, we may have to enter the town."

"Chico," Jose said, because he had just heard the words he'd been hoping he would not, "that is Red Sand."

"I know what town it is, cabron!" Chico snapped. "If I decide that we will go into town, then that is what we will do."

"Of course, Chico, of course," Jose said.

"Tell the others."

"I will tell them," Jose said. "They will go wherever you tell them."

"And you, Jose?"

Jose looked at his leader and said, "Of course, Chico. I go where you go."

"Make camp, then, and we will wait until morning and see."

As Jose did as he was told Chico stared down at the town of Red Sand and wondered if all that money was down there someplace. Perhaps the gringos would all kill each other, and then Chico Mendez would become a very rich man.

At that point, of course, he would have to get rid of Jose and the others. There was no point in sharing *his* wealth with them.

No point at all.

Jud Barlow returned to Red's room and told him the same thing Jim and Steve had said just moments before.

"I can't find them anywhere, Red."

"Do you think they left town?" Jim asked.

"Don't be an ass, Jim," Red said. "There's no reason for them to leave town. If they're not in any of the cantinas turning their noses up at the men in this town then they must be back in their rooms. Forget it and get out, now. I'm turning in."

"I'm going back to my gals," Steve said.

"Steve—" Jim said, looking at his brother.

Steve returned the look and then said, "Yeah, all right, Jim, come on."

Jim smiled broadly and trotted after him.

Jud turned toward Red and then, interpreting his oldest brother's look, proved that he wasn't totally dull after all.

"I know," he said, "the roof."

Heck finished taking care of his horse—who knew how long *this* one would have to last—and then spread out his bedroll. He checked his gun, then lay down with the holster on, his rifle by his side, and his head on his saddle. He knew that the slightest sound would bring him instantly awake.

Tomorrow, he thought, maybe this will all come to a head.

[31]

When Tracker awoke the next morning there was a bobbing head between his legs and a darting tongue on his swollen cock.

"Bonnie?"

"Who else would it be?" she asked, looking up at him. "Did you think Tess would sneak in here?"

"I don't know your sister well enough to answer that question," Tracker said, and then added, "or you, for that matter."

"Believe me, Tracker," Bonnie said, "Tess and I each took our choice, and you were mine."

"The feeling is mutual."

"Not yet," she said, "but it will be..."

He didn't know what she meant, but caught on as she swung around and lay down atop him with her face in his crotch and her crotch in his face. He had never encountered this position before, but immediately saw its benefits.

As she took his cock in her talented mouth he leaned forward slightly and ran his tongue along her moist, warm slit. When he slid his tongue between her wet lips to dart inside her, she moaned around his rigid shaft, and the vibrations this caused through his cock were incredible.

He put his hands on her hips and sucked on her while she bounced her butt against his face at exactly the same tempo her head was bobbing up and down as his cock slid in and out of her mouth.

He wondered what kind of night Wes had spent with little sister Tess.

* * *

Tess had awakened Wes in much the same way that morning, but instead of staying in bed she took him down the hall to the bathtub.

"I have to have a bath in the morning," she told him, "but it's much more fun if I'm not alone."

"I see," Wes said, following her into the room, "just any fella would do, huh?"

"Wes, you are not just any fella, believe me," Tess said, pulling at his pants, which he'd slid on for the walk down the hall.

In moments they were both naked and in a tub of hot water—but this was nothing like the hot water he and Tracker would find themselves in later that day.

"What goes with Tracker?" Bonnie asked as she dressed beside him.

"What do you mean?" Tracker asked, buckling his gunbelt.

"I mean is that a first name or a last name or what?" Bonnie explained.

"That's it," Tracker said. "That's all I need."

"Just Tracker, huh?"

"Isn't Tracker enough?"

She grinned and ran her tongue around her lips lasciviously and said, "More than enough."

He slid his arms around her waist and kissed her long and hard.

"We'd better go and get some breakfast before we end up back in bed," she said, and then with a pained look added, "I don't think I could take it."

"You can take it, all right," he assured her, "and you can dish it out. And what about you?"

"What about me?"

"What goes with Tess and Bonnie?"

"Tracker goes pretty well with Bonnie, I can tell you that—"

"I mean a last name."

"Oh, well I don't mind telling you *my* whole name. Tess and I are Barlows."

Tracker stopped short and stared at her.

"Barlow?"

"That's right."

"Your last name is Barlow?"

Looking puzzled she said, "That's what I said. What's wrong, Tracker?"

"Nothing," he said, quickly. He needed some time to think this one over and talk to Wes—if Wes hadn't skipped town while Tracker was otherwise involved during the night. "Nothing at all. I, uh, I met a couple of your brothers last night, that's all. They are your brothers, aren't they? I mean, they're not..."

"Our husbands? Hell no, they're our brothers, all right, and that's enough of a burden, thanks. Which ones did you meet?"

"One with red hair and another who has a quick fuse."

"Red and Jim. Get along with them?" she asked with genuine interest.

"I don't know about Red, but I almost had to... quiet your brother, Jim."

"What happened?"

"Red stepped in."

"Red's like our daddy since our parents died," she explained. "You're lucky you didn't come up against Jud."

"Why is that?"

"You'll see when you meet him. He just may be one of the few men around that even you would have to look up to."

"Really? Well, I'm looking forward to that."

"Just remember one thing."

"What? Don't get him mad?"

She shook her head and said, "Jud doesn't get mad."

"Then what's to remember?"

"Don't get Red mad," she warned, "because as gentle as Jud is, he'll do whatever Red tells him to do."

"Even violence?"

She stared at him seriously and said, "Even murder."

[32]

Tracker and Wes went to breakfast with Bonnie and Tess, but not before Tracker managed to have a brief conversation with his partner.

"They're what?" Wes asked.

"They're Barlows," Tracker said.

"Wives?" Wes asked, carefully.

Tracker shook his head and said, "Sisters."

Wes breathed a sigh of relief and said, "That's a relief. We've got enough problems with the Barlows without spending the night with their wives."

"That's for sure, but the way it stands now it could work to our advantage."

"How do you figure that?"

"Well, first, the girls just might know where the money is and second, maybe the brothers will think twice about moving against us when they see how... involved we are with their sisters."

"It could work another way, too," Wes said. "They might come after us *because* we're with their sisters."

"Well, that's a chance we'll have to take in order to find that money."

"Tracker, let me ask you this."

"What?"

"Would you take the money without the Barlow boys?" Wes asked.

"You're not asking me that just because we spent the night with their sisters."

"No, I'm asking you for your priorities."

"*My* priority is the money, Wes."

"Then that's my priority, too. Let's go get it."

They started by having breakfast with Bonnie and Tess.

127

The girls picked out a small cafe run by a husband and wife of equal girth. The four were consuming a hearty breakfast when Red Barlow walked in, followed by Jim. Tracker recognized them both from the confrontation in the cantina the night before.

"Bonnie," Red said, looking down at his sister.

"Good morning, Red."

"Who are your friends?"

"You've met them," Bonnie said, "last night in the cantina."

"Oh, yeah," Red said, "I remember. I saved Jim from being taken apart by this big fella here."

"Tracker," Tracker said.

"Mr. Tracker, I'm Red Barlow, and this is my brother, Jim."

"Uh huh."

"Bonnie, I'd like to talk to you," Red said to the older of his two sisters.

"After breakfast, Red, all right?"

Red stared at his sister, who turned away and looked across the table at Tracker. Tracker expected the man to insist, but instead he backed off.

"All right," Red Barlow said, "but right after breakfast, Bonnie."

"Of course."

Red Barlow jerked his head toward Jim who, after glaring murderously at Tracker, obediently followed his brother out.

Tracker couldn't believe what he'd just witnessed, but it gave him an idea that he wanted to discuss with Wes—and Heck Thomas.

"That's your older brother, huh?" Tracker asked.

"Yeah, he's like a father to us all—but there are times when he can get a little pushy."

"You told me not to get him mad, though."

"Oh, Tracker," Bonnie said, exchanging smiles with her sister, Tess, "you couldn't get him mad, but we can. I mean, Jud wouldn't lay a hand on us, and neither would any of the other boys. They'd be lost without us."

"I see," Tracker said, exchanging fleeting glances with Wes.

The look on Wes's face was enough to tell Tracker that they were thinking along the same lines, now all

128

they had to do was get together with Heck and talk it over.

As soon as Heck got to town.

As Red and Jim Barlow stepped out onto the board-walk in front of the cafe they saw the stranger riding down the main street of Red Sand.

"What do you make of that?" Jim asked.

"I don't know," Red said, peering at the lone man, "but three strangers in two days just don't sit right with me."

"What are we gonna do?"

"Get ahold of Jud and Steve. We're gonna find out who he is. Let's go."

Tracker and Wes left the girls in the cafe, saying that they wanted to check on their hotel rooms and their horses.

"You're not thinking about leaving town already, are you?" Bonnie asked Tracker, laying her hand on his arm and squeezing.

"Leaving?" Tracker repeated, playing his hand over hers. "I'd have to be crazy to think about leaving now, wouldn't I, Wes?"

"Crazy," Wes agreed.

"See?" Tracker said, looking at Bonnie.

"Uh huh," Bonnie said, exchanging glances with Tess.

"Besides, we don't have enough money to get us very far," Tracker said.

"If money's the problem—" Tess began, but Bonnie gave her a glare that cut her off. The exchange only served to strengthen the hunch Tracker was working on.

"Wes?" Tracker stood up.

"Yeah, coming," Wes said, and rose to his feet.

"We'll see you ladies a little later, then," Tracker said.

"If you don't," Tess replied, glancing at Wes, "we'll come looking for you."

"We'll take that as a promise," Wes told her, smiling. Tracker pushed him toward the door.

Outside, they stopped at the boardwalk and Wes said, "What was that all about?"

"You're thinking the same thing I'm thinking, ain't you?"

"I might be," Wes affirmed. "Why don't you tell me what you're thinking and then I'll tell you if it's the same thing I'm thinking?"

"I'm thinking that it might not be Red Barlow who controls the Barlow purse strings, Wes, that's what I'm thinking. What are you thinking?"

"The same thing."

"Right."

"So what do we do?"

"We find out, that's what we do," Tracker said. "You heard Tess before Bonnie shut her up. 'If money's the problem,' she said. It's not, for them."

"And we saw the way Bonnie talked to Red, and the way Red backed down."

"You know what that tells me?"

"What?"

Tracker started laughing then and said, "Jesus, I don't believe this." He looked totally amused by whatever he was thinking.

"Want to let me in on it?" Wes asked.

"That tells me," Tracker said, very deliberately, "that Bonnie—and maybe Tess, too—knows where the money is, but Red and the others don't. It's *got* to be the girls controlling the purse strings. Don't you see?"

Wes looked straight ahead for a while and then said, "Yes, I guess that fits."

"We've got to talk to Heck," Tracker said quickly. "He was supposed to ride in this morning."

"Maybe he did," Wes said.

They looked at each other and then Tracker said, "The livery."

A few moments later, when Bonnie and Tess Barlow came out of the cafe, they saw their four brothers striding purposefully down the main street toward the livery.

"What do you suppose that's about?" Tess asked.

"I don't know," Bonnie said, "but Tracker and Wes said they were going to check their horses, didn't they?"

"Yep."

"I think our brothers are about to get protective again," Bonnie said, wearily.

"We'd better get over there before someone gets hurt."

"That's for sure."

When Tracker and Wes reached the livery Heck was unsaddling his own horse.

"What's the matter," Wes called out, "you don't trust the liveryman?"

Heck looked up at them and said, "I'm expecting company. I told him to get lost."

"Company?" Tracker frowned.

"As I rode in there were two men in front of this little cafe watching me. They were Americans and they looked real interested."

"The Barlows," Wes said.

"If they find us here together—" Tracker started to say, but there was no need for him to finish the statement. They all knew what it would mean.

Wes moved back toward the livery stable doors and peered out.

"Too late," he called out, "here they come—all four of them. Jesus, that Jud is a monster!"

"All right," Tracker said, "we'll have to try and bluff it out. We told the girls we were going to check on our horses, so let's check them."

He and Wes moved toward their animals and were in their stalls when the Barlows all entered.

"Can I help you?" Heck asked as they walked in.

"We're the welcoming committee," Jim Barlow said, grinning.

"Shut up," Red snapped. Red was not looking at the stranger, however, he was looking past him to the stall where Tracker was standing, his height making him clearly visible.

"You boys know each other?" he asked aloud.

"Who?" Heck asked. He turned and looked at Tracker

and said, "You mean that fella?" Shaking his head he added, "He's a stranger to me. Came in and said something about checking his animal."

"I'm checking mine, too." Wes stepped out of his stall. "Anything wrong with that?"

Tracker wished Wes had kept his mouth shut, but the damage was done. He stepped out of Two-Pair's stall and faced the Barlows with Wes and Heck.

"Is there a problem here?"

Red looked at the three of them in turn, and then settled on Tracker.

"I find it real disturbin' to have three strangers ride into this town in two days, is all," Red said. "You fellas all on the run?"

"On the run from what?" Heck asked.

"Anything."

"Who's askin'?" Heck inquired—as if he didn't know.

Grim-faced, Red replied, "I am."

"Come to think of it," Tracker said, "we didn't actually get around to names last night, did we?"

"Don't tell me my sisters didn't fill you in, friend?" Steve asked.

"The only question is, which is which," Tracker said.

"I'm Red Barlow," Red said, "that's all you need to know."

"Well, I'm Tracker," Tracker said, "and that's all I've got a mind to tell you." Tracker turned to Wes and said, "My horse looks all right."

"Mine, too."

Tracker turned back to Red and said, "Then we'll be leaving."

"Jud," Red said.

Jud Barlow moved to block their path and said, "My brother don't want you to leave."

"Oh? Why not?"

Jud frowned at the question, then looked at Red and said, "Why not, Red?"

Red frowned at his overgrown brother and then spoke to Tracker.

"I'd like to know why the three of you are here."

"Well, I can't speak for this fella here," Tracker said, indicating Heck Thomas, "but for me and my partner here—it's none of your business."

Red's jaw stiffened and he said, "I'm making it my business."

"Look," Heck said, "you fellas seem to have some kind of personal beef, so I'll be moseying—"

"Jud!"

"My brother Red, he don't want you to leave," Jud told Heck.

"You better get this big baboon out of my way," Heck said, eyeing Jud up and down.

"You fellas must think I'm stupid," Red said.

"You must be a mind reader," Wes said.

Red narrowed his eyes this time and said, "Three strangers don't ride into Red Sand at the same time unless they're together."

"We didn't ride in at the same time," Tracker pointed out. "We came in on different days."

"In Red Sand, that's the same time," Red Barlow said. "I want to know why you're here."

"What are you worried about, Barlow?" Tracker asked. "You think we're law?"

"You don't look like law—but that don't mean you ain't."

"If I was why would I be here?"

"For the money," Jim Barlow said, and Red threw him a nasty look.

"Shut up, you idiot!"

"Red, don't call me—" Jim started to say, but Steve nudged him into silence.

"Tracker," Wes said, "I think we ought to lay our cards on the table, seeing as how we're all here."

"Wes—"

"You've got to understand these people, Tracker," Wes went on. "All they understand is the truth—ain't that right, boys?"

"You talk too much for a man with an empty gun," Heck said, and Tracker threw him a look that said "Look who's talking."

"All right," Red said, "let's see you lay your cards on the table." He looked at Wes and said, "You seem to want to do all the talking."

"Not all of it," Wes said amiably, "just enough."

"Then get started."

134

"Oh, I think maybe I'll wait a few seconds for the ladies to join us."

Everyone looked toward the door then, as Bonnie and Tess walked in.

"What's going on, Red?" Bonnie demanded.

"Nothing that concerns you," Red said. "Take your sister and get back to your boarding house."

"Red, stop giving orders," Bonnie said.

"Bonnie—"

"You better listen to your sister, Red," Tracker said, "or she won't tell you where she hid the money."

Now all heads turned toward Tracker.

"What are you talking about?" Red demanded.

Before Tracker could answer, Jim blurted, "How did you know—"

"Goddamn it, Jim, shut the hell up!" Red bellowed.

"It's too late now, Red," Bonnie said. "Stop shouting at him. You know he acts even dumber when you do that."

Bonnie stepped in front of her brothers to face Tracker, thumbs hooked in her belt.

"So you're here for the money, huh?"

"That's what I was hired for," Tracker said. "To get it back."

"Hired?" Heck said, looking at Tracker.

"Surprises all around, huh?" Wes asked, grinning at Heck.

"You shut up."

Tracker, Heck and Wes stared at the six Barlows and the tension started to thicken in the air.

"Tracker," Bonnie said, breaking the silence, "what happened to Jesse?"

"He's dead."

"How'd that happen?" Bonnie asked, holding up a hand to keep Red from speaking.

"I broke him out of jail and he got shot while we were escaping."

"Why'd you break him out?"

"So he could bring me here."

"He wouldn't have!" Red snapped.

"You're probably right," Tracker said, "but I figured it was worth a shot."

135

"You planned to let him get away from you so you could follow him here anyway, right?" Bonnie asked.

"You really are the brains of this family, aren't you?" Tracker said.

Bonnie ignored the remark.

"What happens now?" she asked.

"Now I have to take the money."

"My brothers aren't going to let you do that," she said. "Not without killing somebody."

"I'd prefer not to."

"How much is the bank giving you to bring the money back?"

"Ten percent."

"Ten percent," Bonnie said, nodding.

"How much is that?" Jud asked.

"Ten percent!" Heck demanded.

"How much is that?" Jud asked, again.

"That's what he said, Heck," Wes said, still grinning. "Ten percent."

"How much is—"

"Sixty thousand dollars?" Heck Thomas said, staring at Tracker.

"I was going to give you some," Tracker said.

"Sure," Heck said.

"And you can take the credit for bringing it back," Tracker added. "All I want is my money."

"Well, to get your money," Bonnie said, "you've got to take our money. You figure you and your friends can do that?"

Heck finally began to regret his remark about Wes's empty gun.

[34]

Tracker considered Bonnie's question for a few seconds and then said, "Well, I reckon I'd have to try."

"What about your friends?"

"That's up to them."

Bonnie looked at Heck, who said, "I've come this far. Besides, I've got to keep him alive so I can break his neck."

"And you?" she asked Wes. "With the empty gun?"

"Even with an empty gun I'm better than most men," Wes said confidently. "I'll stay."

"That's it, then," Tracker said. "Bonnie, you'd better take Tess and go outside."

Bonnie stared at Tracker, then shook her head and said, "There's enough money to go around, Tracker."

Before Tracker could reply Red stepped forward and pulled Bonnie by the arm.

"Like hell there is, Bonnie!" he snapped. "Do what the man said and get outside. Jud!"

"Come on, Bonnie," Jud said, taking her by the arm. On the way to the door with her in tow he collected Tess's arm and walked them both outside. He came back in without them.

"How do you want to do this?" Tracker asked.

"We're gonna kill you!" Red said. "If it wasn't for you, Jesse'd be alive now."

"And in jail."

"But he'd be alive, which is more than I can say for you in a few minutes."

"Who's the gunhand here?" Wes asked.

"Me," Steve said, taking a step forward.

"Good?"

"Real good."

"What about Jud?"

They all looked at Jud, who wasn't even wearing a gun.

"I don't need no gun," he said slowly.

"Red, if we start shooting he's going to be the first one to get killed."

"Come on, Red, let's get it over with," Jim said.

He went for his gun, but before anyone else could move Wes drew and fired in the blink of an eye. The bullet went through Jim's right shoulder and if he'd had time to draw his gun he would have dropped it.

All eyes moved to Wes, the man who was supposed to have been wearing an empty gun.

He looked at Tracker, shrugged and said, "When we went into the stalls I took the liberty of taking some bullets from the belt and loading the gun. I figured I might need it."

"Looks like you figured right," Tracker said. "That's a mighty quick move you got there," he added, and in that moment he put it all together in his head. All the different names Wes had used, and that move.

Red took a step and Wes brought his gun to bear on the oldest of the Barlows.

"It's over, Red," he said. "I didn't kill Jim, but I could have. I could kill all of you, too, if I want."

"It don't matter," Red said. "You ain't got the money, and you ain't gonna find it."

"That may be," Wes said, "but we've got you and your brothers."

"Do you?" Red asked. "Jud!"

"Sure, Red," Jud said. He looked at Wes and started toward him.

"Make him stay back, Red," Wes said, pointing his gun at the big man.

When Red didn't react, Tracker did.

"Hold it, Jud," he said, stepping between him and Wes's gun.

"Get out of my way."

"Move, Tracker," Wes said.

"Don't shoot him, Wes."

"Mister, if you don't move I'll have to move you."

"Jud, it's all over."

"Not 'til Red says."

138

"Jud!" Bonnie called from the door. "Move back, Jud."

Jud turned his head in his sister's direction and said, "Not 'til Red says."

In that moment Tracker drew his gun and laid the barrel alongside Jud's head. The big man grunted, stepped back and looked at Tracker, then shook his head in an attempt to clear it. Blood flowed from the cut on his scalp. Tracker brought his gun around again and it cracked against Jud's jaw, dropping the man to the ground.

"Damn it—" Red said. He went for his gun, and Steve followed.

"Red, no!" Bonnie shouted.

Wes swung his gun around and shot Steve in the chest. Tracker dropped and fired at the same time as Heck, both of their shots thudding into Red's torso.

"Jim, don't!" Tracker said as Jim tried to reach his gun with his left hand.

Bonnie hurried to Jim's side and grabbed his arm. Tess came in after her and stared at her fallen brothers.

"It's over, Jim," Bonnie said.

"No it ain't," Jim said. "Don't give him the money, Bonnie."

"What good's the money now?" she asked. "Jesse, Red, Steve, they're all dead. There's only us, Jim, and Jud."

"Jud," Tess said. She rushed to her brother and bent over him. "He's alive," she said to Bonnie in relief.

"Collect the guns, Heck," Tracker said, holstering his. He moved toward Bonnie and said, "What about the money, Bonnie?"

"It's at the boarding house," she said, "under a loose floorboard in my room. Take it and get out. Leave us be."

Tracker knew that he *could* have taken Jim and Jud back with him and turned them over to the law, but he didn't think it was necessary. He looked at Heck for confirmation.

"The money's enough," Heck said.

"That's it, then," Tracker said. "Let's help the girls get their brothers over to their rooms and collect the money. We've still got one problem to solve before we leave town."

"Chico," Heck said.

"Yeah," Tracker agreed. "Chico."

When Chico saw Tracker carrying several saddle-bags across the main street toward the cantina, he said, "He has found it." He turned to his men and announced, "Mount up. We are going into town to collect our debt."

Chico, Jose and the others rode into town bold as you please and stopped their horses in front of the cantina. Chico was convinced that a show of force would convince the gringos to turn over the money.

"Señor!" he shouted. "Come out, please, and bring my money!"

When there was no reply he called, "Por favor, señor, you are making it harder on yourself."

"Actually," a voice said, from above them, "I'm making it harder on you!"

The Mexicans looked up and saw Tracker on the roof, leisurely pointing a rifle at them.

"You are one man against four," Chico said, spreading his hands and shrugging. "You cannot hope to avoid dying if you choose to fight us. Please, for all our sakes, be reasonable. Throw the money down."

"I've got a better idea," a voice said from inside the cantina. Chico lowered his eyes and saw a gun pointing at him from a window of the cantina. It was in the hand of Heck Thomas. "Why don't you and your friends throw down your guns."

"Sounds like a good suggestion to me," another voice said from behind them, and across the street stood Wes with his gun—fully loaded.

"You were too cocky, Chico," Tracker called down from the roof.

"Cocky?" Chico repeated, frowning in puzzlement. "What does that word mean, señor?"

"It means drop your guns, or we'll drop you, señor," Tracker said. "That's what it means."

[35]

Back in Huntsville Tracker and Heck Thomas met in the Huntsville Saloon to settle up.

"You didn't tell me that you were working for the bank," Heck complained.

"That's because no one was supposed to know," Tracker explained.

"Uh huh."

"You want to complain?"

Heck thought it over a moment then said, "Actually, I guess I don't have a lot to complain about, do I? It was you who got the bank to give me a one percent fee, wasn't it? Six thousand dollars is more than I've ever had at one time in my life."

"Take care of it," Tracker warned, "because it won't last forever."

"You should know, I guess," Heck said. "You've probably handled much more than I have."

"I've had my share, I guess, but it goes almost as quickly as it comes."

"You also told the bank to give me all the credit, didn't you?"

"Well, it wouldn't do me any good to get *my* name all over the newspapers, would it?" Tracker said. "That's not the way I do business."

"I guess not. I guess neither one of us has much to complain about," Heck said, "but what about Wes?"

"I guess you'll know that before I will," Tracker said. "I'm heading back to San Francisco. When you find out what they decide to do with him, will you let me know?"

"I'll send you a telegram, you can count on it," Heck Thomas promised. "When are you leaving?"

Tracker looked down at his empty beer mug and said, "Right after you buy me one more drink.

[Epilogue]

Tracker was in his room with Shana when the telegrams came.

To be more accurate, Tracker had his head between Shana's legs, her bristly red bush rubbing his chin raw as he licked her avidly.

That was when the knock came at the door.

"Oh, Jesus—" Shana cried out, and he wasn't sure if it was because she was close to her orgasm, or because of the knock on the door.

"Don't—" she said, grabbing his head so that he wouldn't get up.

"Take it easy," he said, giving her a last flick of his tongue before calling out, "Who is it?"

"Telegrams."

The voice was not familiar so he called out, "Slide them under the door."

There was a pause and then the voice said, "Okay, Mr. Tracker."

The telegrams slid beneath the door and Tracker yelled, "Find the manager and tell him I said to give you a big tip!"

"Thank you!"

The telegrams remained on the floor while Tracker reapplied himself to what he'd been doing before he was interrupted...

"Jesus, what a time for a telegram to arrive," Shana said sometime later.

"That's right, I did get a telegram, didn't I?" Tracker said. "Thanks for reminding me."

He got up off the bed and she watched, surprised as always at how gracefully he moved, even when totally naked. It took a special kind of man to be graceful without clothes.

He picked up the two telegrams from the floor and sat on the bed with them.

The first one was from Heck Thomas. It said, very briefly: WES TO SERVE FULL TERM. NO PARDON. BAD DEAL. HECK

"Damn," Tracker said.

"Bad news?" Shana asked, making no attempt to read over his shoulder.

"It's not good."

When he didn't elaborate Shana leaned back against the pillows and decided to wait. Whatever was in those two telegrams was Tracker's business, and he rarely discussed that with anyone.

The second telegram was from the Huntsville Penitentiary. It was even more brief.

SEE YOU IN TEN YEARS.